Antonietta Klitsche de la Grange

The Last Days Of Jerusalem

Antonietta Klitsche de la Grange

The Last Days Of Jerusalem

ISBN/EAN: 9783741189203

Manufactured in Europe, USA, Canada, Australia, Japa

Cover: Foto ©Andreas Hilbeck / pixelio.de

Manufactured and distributed by brebook publishing software (www.brebook.com)

Antonietta Klitsche de la Grange

The Last Days Of Jerusalem

THE

LAST DAYS OF JERUSALEM

BY

MADAME A. K. DE LA GRANGE.

TRANSLATED FROM THE SECOND ITALIAN EDITION.

NEW YORK:

P O'SHEA, PUBLISHER,

45 WARREN STREET.

PREFACE.

THIS present sketch will not be uninteresting nor useless to our readers, the more so as under the graceful form of a story, enlivened by numerous episodes cleverly introduced by the authoress, it is in reality a page of fully authenticated history. The dissolution of the Jewish nation and its capital reduced to a mass of ruins and ashes, was an event of the utmost importance to Christianity, as it was the terrible but literal fulfilment of the prophecy of Jesus Christ; and one among a thousand others which constitutes a proof of his Divinity. We are told by cotemporary writers, as well as by the Jews themselves, of the terrible atrocities committed in the very heart of Jerusalem while it was besieged by the forces of Titus; and also that notwithstanding the precautions taken by the Roman general to ensure the safety of the Temple, that wonder of the universe, it nevertheless fell a prey to inextinguishable flames. When we read that countless numbers

of Jews perished during this war, and that more
than ninety-seven thousand were transported into
other lands, and sold like beasts at public auction
how can we help believing in the Divine wisdom
of Jesus, who, about forty years before these occur-
rences, had distinctly foretold them? To those who
showed Him the Temple, telling Him that it was
adorned with goodly stones and gifts, He said:
"These things which you see, the days will come in
which there shall not be left one stone upon a stone
that shall not be thrown down. . . . Woe to them
that are with child and give suck in those days:
for there shall be great distress in the land, and
wrath upon this people; and Jerusalem shall be
trodden down by the Gentiles." *

We need add no more in commendation of this
book in which the authoress has contrived to popu-
larize a really classical though somewhat ignored
event, and to render it agreeable and interesting to
those who do not pay much attention to history.

Luke xxi. 5, 6, 23, 24.

CONTENTS.

THE LAST DAYS OF JERUSALEM.

CHAPTER I.

THE HUT OF LAKE ASPHALTITES.

It was sunset; and the sun declined gradually, hiding the half of its disk behind the rugged mountains which from the fruitful land of Jericho branch out beyond the barren shores of Lake Asphaltites. All was buried in profound silence; and the last rays of the retreating orb of day illumined with rosy light the brackish waters of the lake and the foul sands which surround it. The evening breeze did not refresh the air heated by the scorching effects of a summer's day, and in that cursed spot nature appeared covered with a mourning veil. The high mountains which border the vast plains surrounding the Dead Sea and extend even to Zoab, seemed blacker than ever, and from the effects of the retreating light looked like fiery volcanoes in full eruption.

However, amid that deathlike silence, through that vast solitude, lying as it were under the malediction of Heaven, walked a young girl of about twenty years of age, unaccompanied save by a lion, which followed her with slow and majestic steps.

The maiden was tall and slight in figure, and her face, bronzed by the tropical sun, was of the pure Hebrew type. Her mouth was small, and her parted lips showed the white ivory of her teeth; her nose, slightly aquiline, gave an expression of energy to her features without diminishing their beauty; but that expression, which at first sight seemed almost stern, was partly mitigated by the angelic sweetness of her black eyes adorned by long eyelashes. Her clothing consisted of a long gray woollen tunic with a rope for the girdle. A bandage, also of wool, was wrapped around her head, hiding all her thick hair, which rendered her head-dress still more enormous; and her little feet wore heavy sandals with wooden soles fastened to her legs with cords formed of rushes. A basket made of dried palm-leaves hung on her right arm, filled with exquisite fruit, which shed a delicious perfume around her.

She was walking hastily towards the southern part of the lake, occasionally turning her head, now towards Jericho, from which she was every moment

withdrawing further, and now towards Jerusalem
Of what was she thinking as she sadly watched th.
two cities?

Perhaps she thought of the land where the sweet
scented Cytisus * raises its triangular stem, and
where the incorruptible rose † grows flourishingly,
irrigated by the waters rendered fruitful by the
blessing of the prophet Eliseus. Or possibly, when
turning her eyes towards Sion, she saw mentally
the besieging camp before its walls, and with the
fervid imagination of twenty, perceived the tents of
the enemy and the shining armor of the oppressors
of Judea.

No, she thought not of that. Neither the flowers
nor the fruitful waters of Jericho could win a
smile from her lips, since misfortune had saddened
her heart. Nor did she think upon the Roman
army; her mind wandered towards the land where
lay the bones of her mother; that land which, driv-
ing her from her bosom, had forced her to seek the
solitude of the desert in company with her gray-
haired father.

The evening drew on, and the girl quickened her

---

* The Cytisus is a triangular shrub bearing flowers upon the top of the
stalk.
† The rose of Jericho resembles the flowers of the elder-tree, and has no
fragrance, but is distinguished from other plants by its incorruptibility.

1*

steps in order to reach the end of her journey; passing rapidly along, she glanced furtively at the waters of the lake, which, no longer illumined by the reflection of the sun, had resumed their natural .eaden hue.

For some distance the traveller pursued her way along the shores of Lake Asphaltites; then turning towards the east, she walked in the direction of a group of trees scarcely perceptible in the distance; and as night set in she reached a small oasis, which seemed a very Eden amid the barrenness of the desert.

A few dwarf palm-trees were scattered here and there over a small space of ground, and some tropical plants with sharp yellowish leaves grew with some difficulty, appearing however most luxuriant to the eyes of the wanderer accustomed to the sterility of the interminable desert. Three heaps of stones, arranged in a triangular form, served as a wall for a well, not far from which stood a hut built of trunks of palm-trees and covered with a mat of rushes.

The maiden stopped upon the threshold of th miserable dwelling and sighed deeply, then raising her eyes towards heaven, entered the house, whilst the lion lay down near the well.

The interior of the hut bore the appearance of the greatest poverty; a mat divided it into two parts. In the outer part was a mattress of dried leaves covered with a tattered woollen cloth. A rough wooden bench served as a seat; another as a table; and upon the latter stood two earthen vases and a cup. Fastened against the wall were numerous palm-branches, from which hung ripe dates, and opposite the door stood a large cross.

The inner part contained no other furniture save a mattress of leaves and a large stone. Upon the mattress lay an old man clad in a woollen tunic. His snow-white hair hung down upon his breast, mingling with his beard of equal whiteness. He looked wan and meagre; and except for the fever- ish brilliancy of his eyes, which contrasted strangely with the cadaverous expression of his countenance, he might have been taken for a corpse.

He lay motionless with his hands folded upon his breast, occasionally groaning faintly and breathing with difficulty.

The light respiration of the maiden as she bent over his bed roused the invalid from his immo- bility; and raising his head, he said in a faint voice,

"Is that you, Anna?"

Anna kissed the old man's hand, lighted an eai then lamp, and taking a small phial of balsam from her basket gave a few drops of it to the sick man; then seating herself on the ground, pressed her father's hand lovingly, and after kissing it several times, said in gentle tones,

" Father, I would have wished to have had wings to arrive sooner; but you know the road between here and Jericho is by no means short, and I was forced to prolong it to avoid the Roman tents spread out over the plain."

" Did you see Sara ? "

" No, father, five days since she left Jericho for Jerusalem. The poor woman has lost her senses since her spouse has been fighting under the walls of Sion; and forgetful of the danger to which she exposes her children, has hurried thither in search of Joel."

" Imprudent woman ! " interposed the old man, shaking his head.

" Why do you call her imprudent, father ? Have you not frequently told me that the woman should follow her spouse amid the joys and the sorrows of life, in peaceful days as well as in stormy ones ? "

" Yes, my daughter; and in saying that, I was but repeating the words of the Messiah, whose pre .

cepts rendered the woman equal to the man of whom she was formerly but the slave ; but when the duty of a wife clashes with the far holier one of a mother, she should not hesitate in her choice. Separated from Joel, Sara could still have re- mained faithful to him, without exposing her in- fant children to the dangers of a siege. Every thing has its limit here below; and even the purest sentiment becomes guilty, if it be carried to exag geration."

Anna silently bent her head ; and the old man, after a long pause, resumed in a still fainter voice,

" Then Sara did not give you the usual alms ? "

" No, but by her directions, Leah, the old servant. gave me the fruit, the bread, and the balsam."

" Have you any news from Jerusalem ? "

" They are fighting there; and the Romans are victorious, whilst the Israelites yield."

" So it is written : And the valor of the sons of Jacob will be powerless against the will of the Al- mighty. Jerusalem shall fall into destruction ; the owls shall dwell amid its ruins, and the wild beasts shall make their dens therein."

After pronouncing these words, the old man fell back exhausted upon his pillow ; and the girl, thinking upon the prediction regarding her native land, covered her face with both her hands, and wept bitterly.

"Did you learn anything concerning Daniel?" continued the old man.

At this question a nervous shudder shook the frame of the young maiden, who, repressing her emotion with some difficulty, answered:

"I heard nothing . . . Possibly he now lies among the corpses, or is still fighting the Romans, and on the verge of his last moment."

The invalid leaned upon his elbow to look at his daughter, whose pale face had fallen upon her breast, and, laying his long hand upon her head, said to her:

"Do not hide your tears from me, Anna, but weep freely. Do you think, then, that I have not felt your noble sacrifice? You are mistaken if such be the case; for the tears of the children are like darts which pierce the hearts of the parents. Shame has led you to hide your sorrow from all, but your old father has guessed it . . . Daniel was your companion in childhood, and the son of your mother's dearest friend; and I had hoped to close my eyes surrounded by your children; God did not wish it; Daniel closed his eyes to the voice of truth; he knew not the Redeemer predicted by the prophets

and when he offered you, with his hand in marriage, .
the comforts of a wealthy existence, you refused
him to follow your feeble father into the poverty
and privations of the desert. You did your duty,
my child ; but that God who accepted the sacrifice
of an afflicted heart will reward you for it in heaven."

" With you, dearest father, solitude was not painful to me! and if occasionally thinking over the
happy days of my girlhood, a tear trembled on my
eyelids, I looked at your gray hairs, and witnessing
your sorrows, quite forgot my own," answered the
young girl, bathing with tears the hand of the old
man, who went on to say :

" Poor Anna! you have not yet drained the bitter chalice. It grieves me to tell it to you; but
misfortune is less poignant when it is foreseen. You
will soon be left an orphan, having no other de-
pendance upon earth but the faith of Christ, no
other satisfaction save an approving conscience.

At these melancholy words the maiden burst
into loud sobs, and said in a voice interrupted by
tears :

" Oh, father! pray the Almighty to take me with
you to a better world; friendless and fatherless,
what will become of me on this earth?"

"Fear not, beloved Anna! God will not forget

you. Go out of this hut; look at the sky, my child, and you will see it covered with stars whose number you cannot count, but which surpass our own world in size; they revolve in space guided by the hand of the Supreme Creator, who drew them out of gloomy chaos to cause them to shine in the firmament. Look at the insect which crawls over the sand of the desert, or in the slime of the lake, and you will see that it has wherewithal to feed itself; and do you believe then that He who watches over those shining worlds, and takes care even of the insect, will forget the daughter of the man who has had faith in Him. Again I repeat, Anna, you will not be alone; God will watch over the orphan."

The old man ceased; and tired with long speaking, began to breathe gaspingly, joined his hands upon his breast, and turning his head on one side, fell into a feverish slumber.

Anna did not stir through fear of waking her dear invalid, but fixed her tearful eyes upon her father's white hairs, upon that beloved head which was shortly to repose in the tomb. The poor child, repressing her sobs, looked towards Heaven, seeking from God the courage to resign herself to His will. She prayed some time in silence; then, overcome with fatigue, closed her eyes in sleep, but did not

succeed in finding repose; half-awake, a prey to a
nervous wakefulness, she seemed to hear the noise
of the catapults and balistas which tore down the
walls of Jerusalem; she saw the phalanxes of the
Israelites dash victoriously upon the Roman eagles.
Finally leaning her head against the bed, she resolutely closed her eyes, and then nothing was heard
in the hut of Lake Asphaltites but the gentle
breathing of the girl, and the feeble respiration of
the old man, who slept or rather lay in a painful
lethargy.

CHAPTER II.

D**ΛΥ** LIGHT shone over the vast plain surrounding the Dead Sea, when the maiden, awaking, perceived that the old man still slept; walking quietly, to avoid disturbing him, she left the hut, and standing by the open door watched the dense clouds which arose from the lake and vanished into the air. Abandoning herself to grief, the unhappy girl kneeled down to pray for her father, who perhaps might not see the sun set on that evening. After a long and fervent prayer she re-entered the hut, took up a vase in which she used to draw water, and approached the well. Whoever had seen her in her melancholy beauty, walking through that deserted region, would have compared her to Rachel, when, far from the house of Laban, she unexpectedly met Jacob.

At the sight of the young girl, the lion, who was slumbering near the well, shook his mane, and rising, roared as if to welcome his mistress.

It was about four years before, that a caravan

journeying from the far land of Sodom, upon reaching the banks of the Jordan had dropped the lion,
which had been separated from its dam when too
young, on the shores of the Dead Sea, where it
would have died from hunger, had the maiden not
ome to its assistance. Henceforward the beast
grew up in the hut of the desert, and conquering its
ferocious instincts, had become as affectionate as a
dog to its benefactors.

Anna caressed the lion's head, then took up the
vase which she had placed upon the ground, and
sighing deeply, was about re-entering the hut when
she suddenly stopped, grew pale, and uttered an exclamation of surprise at the sight of a man who was
coming towards her.

Accustomed to solitude, the timid girl was terrified at the unexpected appearance of the stranger;
and overcome with fright, fled into the hut, then
regaining her presence of mind she said courageously:

"How foolish my fears are; at a nod Zabul
would devour a man to defend me. . . Possibly it is
some wanderer lost in the desert, and the hut of the
solitaries of the Asphaltites should not refuse hospitality."

So saying, Anna quitted the dwelling, and call

ing Zabul, leaned her shoulder against the rugged
trunk of a palm-tree, and thus awaited the approach of the stranger.

He neither seemed a pilgrim repairing to Jericho,
nor one of the brigands, who, driven from Jerusalem and pursued by the legions of Titus, infested
the desert. He was armed after the Roman fashion : a helmet of tiger skin * covered his head ; a
Spanish sword hung by his right side, † and a shield
covered with leather served him as a buckler.

Anna shuddered at the sight of the Roman ;
although a Christian, she was born in Jerusalem,
and could not overcome the aversion inspired in her
by the invaders who had so long tyrannized over
her country. However, the bearing and gait of the
new-comer appeared familiar to her ; and the nearer
he approached, the more relieved she felt. Suddenly she laid her hand on her heart to still its
beatings, opened her lips to utter a name, but her
voice sank in her throat, and finding it impossible to
speak, she leaned breathlessly against the tree.

* The helmet worn by the Romans was styled *Galerum*, and was made of
the skin of some animal.

† The Roman soldiers wore the sword on the right side, but almost
always fought from a distance, and therefore were provided with seven small
javelins armed with iron points about a palm in length, which they threw
from afar. Nevertheless the historian Flavius Josephus asserts that the
Roman soldiers wore two swords, one on each side, and the longest one
sung on the left flank

The supposed Roman, reaching the spot where she stood, said in a sweet and at the same time sonorous voice:

" Fear not, Anna, it is I."

At the sound of that voice the maiden trembled from head to foot; but repressing her emotion by the force of a powerful will, she said in a slightly tremulous voice:

" You here, Daniel? Clad n the Roman armor? Have you abandoned the w ds behind which your brethren fight, to join the enemy's legions? "

"I am not so vile," answered Daniel, proudly raising his head; then taking off his helmet he threw it on the ground, and crossing his arms, looked with ineffable love upon the maiden, who, pale and trembling, stood before him with downcast eyes.

Daniel was a youth of twenty-seven years of age, of middle height and strong frame. His features were very irregular, but the expression of his countenance inspired sympathy, and his gray eyes were melancholy and dreamy. His hair was of a light chestnut color; and his complexion, although bronzed by the sun, was less dark than the generality of his race. His bearing had a haughty, resolute air, which well suited a Jewish warrior.

The two young people stood opposite each other in silence; finally Anna raised her pale face, which instantly became crimson, and in a voice sweet as that of a girl, began thus:

" What motive brings you into this sandy desert? Did you come to see the descendant of the Asmoneans * expire in the wretched hut to which the malignity of the sons of Jacob has driven him?"

At these words Daniel's face grew pale, anger flashed from his eyes; and knowing not how to vent his wrath, he kicked his helmet, which lay at his feet; then calming himself, he looked sadly at his companion; and once more crossing his arms, said to her :

" You must hate me vastly, if you can believe that the friend of your childhood has become so wicked. No, I did not come hither to rejoice over the death of Simon, but simply to press his hand for the last time ere he sleeps forever in the tomb. I came hither to say to you : Anna, you will soon be left alone in the world; then pray confide your fate to me; I can no longer offer you the peace of a happy existence, now that our country, threatened by the Romans and torn by intestine wars, is about crum-

* The Asmonean, or, to speak more properly, the Maccabean. was the priestly race.

bling under the chastening hand of God. Never
theless, at my side you will be more secure than in
this solitude; and if I should fall in battle, my companions in arms will protect my widow. These are
my reasons for coming. It is now four years since
your father was banished from Jerusalem; my
prayers and threats were useless; the elders appealed
to the Roman Pro-Consul, who was inexorable.
From that moment my thoughts have constantly
followed you in your wanderings. I have frequently
repaired to the borders of the Asphaltites to look
from afar at the hut which sheltered you! The spot
has often echoed to the sound of my sobs! Sara
has often given me news of you; but for some time
I had heard nothing, and wild with anxiety, I fancied you exposed to the constant snares of the Romans; and urged on by despair I eagerly sought
for death! The leader of the invading legions having
accorded three days of truce to the besieged, I strove
so hard that in the end I succeeded in secretly leaving Jerusalem; and, concealing myself under this
detested dress, I came hither to say to you: Anna,
have pity upon me, and grant that I may call you
my wife."

Daniel ceased; and the girl's face, bathed in tears,
evinced the sorrowful emotion which the words of

the young Israelite had awakened in her heart
For a moment she, too, remained silent; then laying her hand upon her heart as if to stay its palpita-
tions, replied, in doleful tones:

"When I shall no longer see my father's white
hairs, nor hear his voice, do you think I shall care
about my future fate?"

Daniel strove to persuade the young girl, but did
not succeed; on the contrary, rejecting every reason, she went on to say:

"I beg you, do not think of me; be satisfied
with Simon's pardon and blessing, and ask nothing
more.   Now wait a little: my father's mind is
weak, and the slightest emotion might prove fatal
to him."

Re-entering the hut, the maiden approached the
sick man, who, opening his eyes, said in a feeble
voice while turning restlessly on his mattress:

" Daughter, my lips are dry, and my breath begins
to fail me."

Anna administered to the old man some few
drops of balsam, then kneeling beside him and
clasping her hands, she said, with some constraint:

" Father, a man has crossed the sands of the des
ert and exposed himself to the danger of death to
come and implore your benediction!"

The old man raised his head from his bed of leaves, cast a bewildered glance around, and asked, anxiously, "Who is he ? "

Anna hesitated to answer. A crimson flush passed over her countenance ; then bending towards her father's ear, she stammered in a low voice the sweet name of Daniel.

"Daniel!" said the old man, and raising himself as if he had suddenly recovered his strength, continued : "Possibly he comes to snatch you from my side, or to speak to you in flattering and guilty language."

Anna besought her father to calm himself, and then narrated to him the manner in which the young Jew had quitted Jerusalem, and, unwilling to lie, did not conceal from him the proposition which he had made to her.

The old man knew Daniel's generous nature, and his first fear, caused only by surprise, having passed away, he became more serene, and desired his daughter to call the young man.

Then Daniel entered the hut, bent one knee to the ground, and said, in a low voice :

"Rabbi,* my heart leaps for joy at the sight of you."

---

* Rabbi in the Hebrew tongue signifies Master.

2

The old man did not answer. He looked at the youth for some moments with truly paternal tender ness, and then said:

"Sit here near me, my son, and talk to me con cerning Jerusalem."

"They are still fighting there, Rabbi; but fruit-lessly, for the Roman eagles triumph, and the chosen people are given up to discord, famine, and pesti-lence. The Israelites are guilty of unheard-of acts; only a mere handful of men fight faithfully for the salvation of the Temple, whilst the greater number headed by John of Giscala and Simon of Jora, abandon themselves to rapine, sacrilege, and every kind of impiety."

"And yet you seek to drag my daughter into this new Babylon," angrily interrupted Simon.

"Anna- will be more exposed to danger in the wilderness than in a besieged city; and when you are no longer living, Rabbi, who will dry the tears of the orphan girl?"

Simon remained for some time in deep medita-tion, and then said, in a tremulous voice, as if agi-tated by some interior struggle:

"Anna, child of that wise woman whom I shall soon rejoin in heaven, I leave the choice freely to you. Will you confide yourself to the Divine pro-

tection, or will you choose a husband with whom to
pass the sad and fleeting days of this life, to be sup-
arated from him throughout eternity? Hitherto I
have spoken to you with the authority of the Divine
precepts; now I will give you no further advice,
but will leave you to the exercise of your own free
will."

Anna turned her eyes from Daniel's face and
fixed them upon that of the old man. A struggle
of sorrowful affections took place within the maid-
en's heart. For a moment she wavered, but the love
of the daughter overcame that of the lover; an expression of heroic energy passed over her sweet
countenance, and extending her hand, she exclaimed
with forced calmness:

"Die in peace, O Simon; your daughter wil
never be the spouse of an Israelite. By the side of
your dying bed I call God to witness to my promise!"

A groan of mingled rage and agony issued from
Daniel's lips; while the old man, clasping his hands,
and looking towards heaven, said in tones of fervent
gratitude:

"Thanks, Omnipotent God! She has come forth
victorious from the trial, and in Thy mercy Thou
wilt not forsake the child of Thy servant."

For a moment the most unbroken silence reigned throughout the hut. Daniel, pale and overcome with grief, had his eyes fixed upon the ground. Anna wiped away the copious tears which she was shedding, and Simeon prayed in a loud voice. At last the latter interrupted his prayer, and, to rouse the young people from their sad reveries, desired his daughter to offer some refreshment to their guest.

Daniel accepted merely a few dates, then prepared to depart; but first, approaching the maiden, said sadly:

"Oh, Anna! do not force me from your presence with my heart deprived of hope and driven to desperation!"

"You heard my promise; I will not be the spouse of an Israelite, but I can become that of a Christian," answered the girl, looking gently at Daniel.

"I will never forsake the faith of my fathers, nore especially when it is trampled upon and oppressed!" said the young man, proudly shaking his head; then laying his hand upon his breast he added bitterly: "This heart was foolish to beat only for you; but never fear, it will soon be cold in death under the walls of Jerusalem."

" You will not die, for death flies from those who seek it," interrupted the old man ; but Daniel did not hear him, for he had rushed forth from the hut.

Anna hid her face in her hands and wept in silence; then she too left the house, and seeing in the distance the retreating form of her lover, sat down and sobbed bitterly. Her tears were no offence against that God who appreciates dolorous sacrifices, and in whose sight virtue is the more sublime and beautiful when it is more difficult to practise. She wept long; but suddenly recollecting herself, she felt remorse for her tears, as if she had forgotten the approaching death of her father, to abandon herself to the compassion inspired by the friend of her childhood. With her heart embittered by this thought she re-entered the hut, and forcing herself to smile at the invalid, hid the cruel anguish which lacerated her heart and caused her to envy the tomb wherein the mortal remains of the descend ant of the Asmoneans would shortly repose.

CHAPTER III.

THE day succeeding the unexpected visit of the young Hebrew, Simon's sickness increased. Lying upon his hard mattress, he breathed with difficulty; and his features gradually losing all expression, his aspect became cadaverous.

Anna constantly remained beside his bed, lavishing every care upon him. Now she would give him some drops of balsam, now moisten his lips with water; frequently she would kneel and rub his extremities with her hands, seeking thereby to revive their vital warmth; but in vain, for the chill of death had already stiffened the limbs of her dying father.

Simon lay motionless, his eyes closed, and a ray of sunlight, piercing through a small aperture in the wall, shone upon his white head, surrounding it as with an aureole of light. Occasionally he opened his half-shut eyes, to look at the only being who was dear to him, and whom he would shortly leave a desolate orphan.

To watch beside the bed of a dying relative or friend is always heart-rending; but still more agonizing when poverty and loneliness prevent us from rendering less painful by material aids the physical sufferings of those who are about leaving this world. Whoever has witnessed death in the wretched dwel lings of the poor, who has seen the tears of a mother or a wife, enduring no less anguish from the approaching death of the beloved invalid than from seeing him lying upon a hard bed which wounds his aching limbs; whoever has seen this, can form some idea of the bitter fate of those who live in indigence and die destitute of every corporal comfort. The sorrow of the survivors of wealthy families is rarely overpowering, and when it is so they can console themselves with the conviction of having done all that they could, humanely speaking, to preserve the life of the beloved deceased; but the poor frequently die from want of care, and their relatives exclaim: " There may perhaps have been some remedy, but we had not the means to purchase it ! "

Such was the case with Anna. The poor child saw her father lie dying upon his miserable bed of dry leaves, and would gladly have given her life to have procured him a softer couch. Agonized by this thought, she raised her eyes to heaven, saying:

"My God, who died upon a cross, forsaken by all and deprived of every comfort, have mercy upon Simon and render his last moments less painful!"

That day the maiden never for one moment quitted the invalid, who had finally lost consciousness. From time to time she spoke to him, but uselessly, for he no longer heard her. At twilight she lighted a small earthen lamp, whose feeble ray, scarcely illuminating the walls of the hut, shone faintly upon her youthful face, which, paled by grief, seemed to picture the agony of the wanderer who, having taken the first step in a thorny path, looks fearfully at the long road which he has yet to traverse; whilst the calm countenance of Simon expressed the contentment of the traveller who, having reached the end of a perilous journey, is delighted to rest himself.

Up to midnight the old man remained motionless, then roused himself, extended his hand in search of a small wooden crucifix which lay near him, and, having kissed it, laid it upon his breast, then called his daughter, who bending over him said gently:

"I am here, father; do you not see me?"

The old man smiled, tried to raise himself, but his strength failed him, and he fell back upon his pillow, saying in a feeble voice which could scarcely be heard,

"Anna, when I am dead, leave the desert and join Sara and Joel; they will protect you. Be faithful to the faith of your father, and do not forget the promise which you made to me."

"Your will shall be accomplished, dearest father," replied the maiden, sobbingly; and clasping her hands she continued, "Father, bless me!"

The aged Christian stretched out his arm, and laying his bony hand upon the young girl's head, uttered a low prayer; then his arm fell upon the couch and he lay motionless as a statue.

Terrified, Anna laid her pale cheek against the old man's lips and was somewhat re-assured upon feeling her father's faint breath. She re-seated herself near the couch, and with anxious look and beating heart watched Simon closely for some time, and perceiving that he slept as sweetly and calmly as a child, hope, that last comfort of the unfortunate, again rose within her soul. Then thinking her father cured, she blessed the Almighty, and unable to overcome the sleep which weighed down her eyelids, she leaned her head upon her breast and slept profoundly.

Towards daybreak she awoke. The lamp had
2*

burned out and the gray light of dawn illumined the hut. The first act of the maiden was to bend towards the invalid, the better to observe him; and she comforted herself on perceiving, as she thought, that the old man was sleeping tranquilly and smiling as if in pleasant dreams; and fearing to disturb so beneficial a repose, she did not move from her place

Meanwhile the day became clearer; the first rays of the sun, penetrating into the hut, enabled Anna to perceive that her father's pallor had increased, and had assumed a cadaverous hue. Tremblingly she laid her hand upon his lips, and finding them icy, cried out despairingly:

"Father, father, answer me!"

Simon did not reply. The soul of the just man had some hours since quitted its mortal tenement! The weary wanderer had passed rapidly through the way of tribulation and now rested in the lap of eternity!

Anna looked at her father's corpse with wandering eyes and convulsed features, called him in agonized tones, begging him to answer her; and ot hearing the beloved voice, uttered shrieks of sorrow. She wept for some time, nature yielding copious tribute of tears to grief, then the wretched girl fell fainting at the foot of the bed of death.

When she recovered consciousness, she rose from
the ground and stood for a moment motionless,
hiding her face in her hands ; then her arms fell by
her sides, and her pale face seemed almost calm ;
despair had been driven from her soul to give place
to Christian resignation.

Approaching her father's corpse, she piously
closed the half-opened eyes, placed the small wooden
crucifix upon his breast, and kneeling beside the
couch remained some time in silent prayer. After
this she seated herself and wept anew, occasionally wiping away her tears, and raising her eyes
towards heaven, she ejaculated :

" Almighty God ! be thou blest in sorrow as well
as in joy ; when thou exaltest as well as when thou
afflictest thy servants ! "

Towards evening the unhappy girl sprang to her
feet in terror at hearing a deep roar, which came
from the threshold of the hut ; she had forgotten
Zabul, who, not having received his usual food, had
come to seek for it.

The maiden left the hut, and shortly returned
with a piece of meat, which she threw to the lion ;
Zabul did not notice it, but with his head bent over
the deceased, smelled him from head to foot, then
roared anew ; and after shaking his shaggy mane,

laid himself down at the foot of the bed of leaves without ever looking at the piece of mutton which was to appease his hunger.*

" You too weep over the death of your master!" said Anna, as she reseated herself to watch beside the corpse.

Throughout the evening and during the whole night, the orphan continued her watch, and the roaring of the king of beasts and the sighs of the maiden formed the dirge of the solitary of Lake Asphaltites.

The morning of the following day still found Anna seated beside the corpse, looking fixedly at it. She spoke to it lovingly, promising it that it should never be parted from her side ; and in her delirium thought not of burying the remains, which had already become corrupted.

After a few more tender words she stooped to kiss the pale face, which seemed as if in a quiet sleep, but drew back immediately, unable to repress the natural repugnance which she experienced upon perceiving that the germ of decay was creeping through the body of her father.

Horrified by the thought she earnestly besought

---

* Whoever believes such sensibility unlikely in a lion, can easily con
vince himself by perusing the "History of the Crusades," by William
Archbishop of Tyre, wherein we find a similar account.

the Almighty that that beloved corpse might remain intact; then convinced of the inutility of her
prayer, she exclaimed amid her tears :

" God will not change the laws of nature in my
behalf! Only on the last day, according to the
vision of Ezekiel, will bone be joined again to bone
and be re-covered with flesh ; now the sand of the
desert must cover the descendant of the Asmoneans
until the day of final judgment."

So saying, full of courageous resignation she
quitted the deceased, and taking up an iron spade
left the hut ; when she passed beyond the group of
palms, she stopped at the foot of a tamarind-tree
which rose loftily amid a quantity of fragrant house-
leeks. She looked sadly at the tree at the foot of
which Simon was accustomed to sit, and like the
Israelites who hung their harps upon the willows
and wept over the captivity of Babylon, she also
groaned over her unfortunate country.

The work of digging a grave was not difficult, for
the ground was extremely soft ; but the poor young
girl, weakened by watching and grief, felt her
strength gradually giving way. Having prepared
the grave, she took from her head the woollen bandage, and folding it in the form of a pillow, placed it
in the bottom ; then entered the hut, raised the

corpse with great difficulty, and burdened with its dead weight walked towards the tamarind-tree ; but as she passed the well a man suddenly issued from behind the group of dwarf palms, and laying one hand upon her shoulder, stopped her progress.

The stranger was still young in years, tall of stature, and robust of limb.　A long black beard hung down upon his breast; his features, of oriental type, bore a pensive and melancholy expression, and his eyes rolled in their orbits like those of a blind man afflicted with amaurosis, the pupils of whose eyes are brilliant but deprived of sight.　However, he was not blind, for he had seen the maiden, and not the slightest expression of his looks could be attributed to indifference for that upon which they fell.　He was clothed like a man of the lowest Hebrew class, wore new sandals, and his rough and calloused hands seemed accustomed to hard labor.

Anna looked fearfully at him, and clasping the beloved corpse to her bosom as if making it her shield, asked tremblingly :

" Who are you ? "

" A traveller who has wandered about from time immemorial," answered the stranger, in a voice faint as though issuing from a tomb.

" We'l, then, continue your journey, and do not

a/nder a daughter from fulfilling a sacred duty,"
naid the maiden, with considerable energy.

"Eternal vengeance directs my steps, and commands me to halt and relieve the weak from the
burdens which oppress them."

So saying, the mysterious man took the corpse
from the young girl's arms, and approaching the
grave, laid it therein; then taking up the spade
from the ground, began to fill up the tomb with
sand.

Anna prostrated herself upon the border of the
grave. Up to that moment, the loss of her father
had not seemed so great, whilst she could yet look
upon his remains; but now that the ground hid
them from her sight, her agony became excessive
and would have driven her to kill herself, had not
religion, the anchor of the unfortunate, spoken to
her mind with its divine language.

The stranger looked at the corpse with an eye of
envy. It seemed as if the sight of death gladdened
his heart. Finally he approached the young girl,
and said to her:

"Cease weeping, O woman! and intone a can-
ticle of thanksgiving; because the descendant of
the Asmoneans no longer cumbers the earth, but is
at rest."

Anna did not hear these words; buried in her grief, she withdrew from the tomb, and went into the hut to take the wooden cross and plant it at the foot of the tamarind-tree; but on her return, she vainly sought the stranger in order to thank him. He had departed, and, walking as if gliding over the sand without touching it with his sandals, was proceeding on his way to Jerusalem.

"This mysterious man terrifies me," said the maiden, turning towards the tomb, and perceiving Zabul, who was lying beside it. "Here," she exclaimed, pointing to the beast, "is the only friend which remains to me upon earth!"

The thought of being alone and thus abandoned in the world, weighed so heavily upon her heart, that it was well for her that she possessed the holy comfort of Christian piety and religion! But, oh! what feelings and affections swelled within her heart at the sight of that simple cross which rose over her father's grave! That sacred sign of human redemption, the sublime monument of the sufferings and death which the incarnate Son of God endured upon this miserable earth, appeared to her surrounded as it were with a celestial light, which dissipated the sombre darkness of her sorrow. She seemed to hear the voice of Him who says

"Come unto me, all ye that labor and are burdened, and I will refresh you!"   She ran to embrace that cross, and watering it with sweet tears, poured out her grief upon it, and found strength, relief, and resignation.

CHAPTER IV.

.AFTER praying for some time at the foot of the cross, Anna returned to the hut, and her grief augmented as she thought of the four years which she had passed there in quiet resignation. In the company of her father, the solitude of the desert had not seemed so frightful as it now appeared to her, and she had endured it courageously in order not to embitter still further his declining years; but now all was at an end for her upon earth. Simon had carried with him into the tomb her every hope, and every link of affection was thus broken for the forsaken orphan.

Agonized by such sad thoughts, she looked at the bed of the deceased, at whose foot she had so often seated herself to listen to words full of faith which taught her to bow her head unmurmuringly to the divine will. But unable longer to bear the sight of that place where every object reminded her of her father, she quitted the hut and walked slowly towards the shore of Lake Asphaltites; reaching there she seated herself upon the ground, and fixed her eyes upon the vast and dreary panorama which presented itself to her view.

The sun had completed the half of its course, and the heavens were veiled with that reddish mist which renders the air still more suffocating in that fiery climate. The two chains of mountains which, stretching along in parallel lines, bordered the land of Sodom, rose blacker than ever, enhancing the light gray shade of the plain, crossed by the river which flowed slowly towards the lake which was to swallow it up.*

A salty crust covered the shores of Lake Asphaltites, whose waters changed their hue according to the reflection of the sun's rays, and which, salter than those of the sea, exhaled a miasma disgusting to the smell and unhealthy beyond belief. Here and there along the sea-shore rose some shrubs richly encrusted with salt, whose fruit, gorgeous and beautiful, symbolic of the enjoyments of this life, enticed the traveller to taste it, only to embitter his lips with the ashes which are contained within its rind.†

The most profound silence reigned around, and

---

* This river is the Jordan, which flows into the Dead Sea.

† Flavius Josephus, in his history of the Jewish wars, as well as Tacitus, in the fourth book of his history, speaks of this fruit.

Anna, seated upon the ground with her hands clasped over her knees, now gazed upon the encircling mountains, witnesses of the miracle mentioned in the sacred Scriptures, and now turned them towards the lake, thinking perhaps to see in the bottom the gigantic shadows of the cities swallowed up by divine wrath,* and her afflicted soul became still more sad; but sadness was dear to her heart, and the smiles of nature and of humanity would have been equally odious to her at this moment.

After watching for some time the waters of Lake Asphaltites, she turned her head towards Jerusalem and uttered an exclamation of surprise at the sight of a distant column of dust ascending towards the sky. Rubbing her eyes, blinded by tears, she looked more attentively, and soon saw that the dust was raised by the feet of several horses, which were galloping towards the lake, and in a few moments a band of Roman knights stopped not far from where the girl was seated.

The commander of the troop sprang from his Arab steed, which stamped the ground impatiently, and having given the rein to one of the knights, approached the banks of the Dead Sea.

---

* According to Deuteronomy four cities were swallowed up by divine wrath, namely; Sodom, Gomorrah, Admah, and Zeboim, which stood formerly in the present site of the Dead Sea.

He was quite young; his dignified bearing and manly features spoke of his natural goodness of heart. His head was covered by a bronze helmet surmounted by an eagle's plume, and furnished with two thin metal plates which, fastening under his chin, served to defend his cheeks. A cuirass of small iron rings linked together covered his heart, and a short tunic lined with purple descended below his knee, leaving exposed his iron greaves. * A sword with the hilt embossed with precious stones, hung by his side; and his hands, delicate like those of a woman, were adorned with rings.

He walked rapidly towards the lake, and kneeling on the ground, scooped up the brackish water in the hollow of his hand, and having brought it to his lips, made a very wry face and exclaimed:

"By Cæsar's camels! the waters of the river Styx cannot be more infernal than these, and I was certainly very foolish to take such a long ride in order to taste them. Decius, call to Terentius to bring me my usual beverage."

So saying, he turned to a knight who had followed him, and who from his vine branch,† which he wore on his right side, seemed to be a centurion.

* According to Polybius the Romans wore only one on the right leg.
† The insignia of a centurion was a vine branch, which he used to strike delinquents.

The latter moved towards the troop* of horsemen, and having spoken a few words to a man-at-
arms, returned to him who seemed to be the head,
bringing a small amphora filled with honeyed wine.†

The youthful warrior eagerly drank the sweet
mixture, but making a fresh contortion, he said:

"By the gods of my country! This wine is
horrible after having tasted that water which savors
of gall. I would give a thousand cestertia for a cup
of fresh water; my throat is parched with the dust
and the heat."

"You will find none here were you to offer in
exchange all the wealth of the Cæsars!" replied the
centurion. But perceiving Anna, he pointed towards her, saying: "There is a woman yonder!
Perhaps she may be the spouse of one of our enemies; let us seize her!"

A flash of anger crossed the speaking countenance
of the youthful commander, who angrily stamped
upon the ground, saying:

"Your proposal is unworthy of a Roman. We
come here to overcome a rebellious people, not to
make war upon women. Were she even the spouse

---

* Every Roman legion consisted of three hundred horsemen, divided into
ten troops and thirty decurias: thirty horsemen composed every troop,
ten every decuria.

† The favorite drink of the Romans was wine mingled with honey.

of John of Giscala, she would be unmolested by me,
and whoever should presume to touch a hair of her
head should be slain by my own sword."

As he spoke, his youthful countenance appeared
still more haughty and beautiful; then he walked
towards the maiden and, unperceived by her, stood
some moments admiring her long black hair, which,
unconfined by the woollen fillet, fell over her shoul
ders, covering them as with a mourning veil; but
finally wearying of his occupation, and urged on by
curiosity, he drew still nearer her to inquire:

"What brings you, maiden, into this dreary soli
tude?"

Anna sprang to her feet, looking wonderingly
on the Roman warrior who stood before her, then
drew back in terror, as if she would seek refuge and
salvation in the depth of the lake.

"Wherefore do you fear?" said the young man,
smiling kindly, and moving further away to re-
assure her. "But tell me," he added, "could you
point out to me a source of sweet water?"

The orphan's first impulse was to give him a decided negative and thus induce him to depart, but her
charity was stronger than her fear. Conquering the
repugnance she felt towards those against whom
Daniel was fighting she pointed towards the spot

where stood the hut, in tones as harmonious as the harp of David:

"Follow me, O Roman."

The warrior did not wait for a second invitation, but at once followed his conductress. Then Anna, after walking entirely around the lake, led him towards the spot where the palm-trees were distinctly visible in the distance.

The centurion walked closely beside his young commander, and seeing that his leader was advancing too far from the troop of horsemen, said to him in a low voice:

"Be prudent; you might fall into some ambush."

At this advice the young warrior shook his head in sign of incredulity, and continued his walk, whilst the centurion muttered between his teeth:

"The sight of a pretty woman makes even the wisest man quite forget his wisdom."

When they had reached the neighborhood of the hut, the Roman leader saw the tamarind-tree at whose foot the cross was planted, and said, turning towards his companion:

"This woman is more of an enemy towards the Israelites than ourselves; for they crucified the Nazarene."

"If she be a Nazarene, do not trust her," said the

centurion, "for the followers of the Galilean who was condemned by Pontius Pilate are sorcerers, and —" Here the centurion suddenly checked himself, and with mingled fear and surprise watched Zabul, who was slowly approaching.

"The companion of my solitude is less ferocious than you imagine," said the orphan, who on turning her head had perceived the terror of the centurion.

The lion, meanwhile, after licking his mistress's hand, as if waiting only a sign from her to spring upon the new comers, turned and laid himself quietly down upon the tomb.

"She is a magician!" cried the centurion, extremely surprised at the docility of the ferocious animal.

Just then Anna stopped on the threshold of the hut, and turning towards the strangers who were following her, said with gentle dignity :

"Accept the meagre hospitality of this poor dwelling, which will be ever open to the inhabitant of Jerusalem as well as to the Roman ; to the Israelite as well as to the Idolater."

Then she entered the hut, and placing a basketful of dates upon the stone which served as a table, invited her guests to refresh themselves.

3

The centurion, with little ceremony, eagerly de. voured the fruit, after first offering it to his companion ; but the latter, refusing it, took merely a cup of fresh water, looking curiously around him as he drank it. The poverty of the place seemed even still great er to his eyes, accustomed as they were to the sybari tic luxury which surrounded the Roman patricians therefore an expression of pity passed over his coun tenance as he thought that so beautiful a maiden was forced to dwell in that wretched abode, while so many others were living in ease and splendor. See-ing poverty thus closely for the first time in his life, he realized how sad a thing it is, and understood that the wealthy, to whom the privation of superfluous goods is a great trial, should do all in their power to enable the poor who surround them to obtain at least the necessaries of life. At the sight of that miserable hut, where the delicate limbs of a woman were forced after a fatiguing day to repose upon a few dried leaves, his heart was filled with that generous pity which was later to crown his short life with glory and hand his name down to the admiration of posterity.

After having examined the dwelling, the warrior approaching the maiden, said inquiringly :

" You live alone in this desert ?"

" Yes, quite alone, since I buried the corpse of my only friend," replied Anna, brushing away with the palm of her hand a tear which shone in her eye.

" Who are you, maiden, lovely as the chaste goddess ?" exclaimed the warrior, overcome by pity at the sight of her sorrow.

" When I invited you under my roof, I did not ask you your name," answered the girl, reprovingly.

" Pardon my indiscretion," said the young man ; then, approaching the centurion, he put his hand into a purse which hung from the latter's side ; and taking thence a quantity of money, offered it to Anna, adding : " Leave this desert, provide yourself with what you need, and when you require money, come to the camp of Titus, and you shall have it in abundance."

The maiden's face grew crimson at his words and action, and pushing away the hand of the enemy of her country, she exclaimed :

" I do not sell the hospitality of the house wherein my father died ! Give your gold elsewhere, Roman ; I should not find use for it."

Her face was so proud and beautiful as she spoke, that the warrior could do no less than look at her with admiration. For a moment both remained silent ; finally the young man took from under his cuirass a small tablet covered with parchment, and wrote several words thereon with an ivory stilus, then handed it to Anna, saying :

"Should you be threatened by the Roman soldiery, who may possibly penetrate even to this solitude, show them this writing and you will be respected ; and by its means you can, if you choose, find asylum and protection within the Roman camp."

Anna took the parchment, and crossing her hands on her breast, bent low in token of gratitude; whilst the warrior, sighing as if in a painful reverie, left the hut saying to himself:

"Who can this maiden be ? She is as beautiful, and yet as haughty as Berenice."

Shortly after the troop of Roman cavalry, amid a cloud of dust, were galloping towards Jerusalem, from whence, during the short interval of truce granted to the besieged city, the youthful commander had departed in order to visit the Dead Sea.

CHAPTER V.

THE loss of persons dear to one is less harrowing
for those who cherish the hope of meeting them in
that blessed country where misfortune, the inseparable companion of the pilgrim upon this earth, does
not embitter those everlasting joys. Whoever does
not believe in eternal rewards and punishments is
as unhappy as he is culpable ; for him, matter min-
gles itself again with matter, and the incorruptible
and immortal spirit dies with the earthly tabernacle
which harbors it. God justly punishes the unbeliever
with the suffering caused him by his incredulity.

Resigned to the divine will and certain of rejoin
ing Simon in the heavenly country, Anna gradually
consoled herself ; but thinking over the best method
of reaching Jerusalem, she shuddered at the idea of
returning to that city from which her father had
been exiled.

Simon sprang from the illustrious race of the
Maccabees, whose family had long held the priesthood and the kingly power. Illustrious by birth and

elevated in intellect, these very high-priests themselves consulted him regarding the laws; and from
his earliest years his voice had been heard in the
synagogue, and he was styled Rabbi even by the
most zealous pharisees.   In his youth, urged on by
curiosity, he had gone up to Calvary to witness the
death of the Son of God, and that blood which redeemed the human race had not spoken to his heart,
buried in the darkness of error; but several years
later the Holy Ghost having by means of an Apos-
tle enlightened his mind, he quitted the synagogue
and received baptism together with his wife and
little daughter.   His conversion could not remain
concealed from his fellow Jews, who for some time
kept silent, meditating vengeance; at last the elders
accused him to the Roman governor as the leader
of a new sect, which, according to them, threatened
to rebel against the power of Rome.   The governor
not having sufficient proofs to condemn him, handed
him over to the people, who, instigated by the pharisees, would have murdered him, had not the voice
of an old Levite somewhat calmed the popular fury.
The convert escaped with his life, but, overwhelmed
with insults, was driven from Jerusalem together
with Anna, on the very day on which his wife had
died after a short and sudden illness.

Not knowing where else to go, the old man and his daughter repaired to Jericho and sought refuge in the house of a young Jew lately married; but the inhabitants learning that Simon was concealed there, crowded round the house, loudly demanding his life. With great difficulty he escaped from his persecu tors. He wandered into the desert and halted by the desolate shores of the Dead Sea, where, far from those who had torn him from the corpse of his beloved spouse, he built the wretched hut in which he died.

Determined to quit the desert, Anna resolved to make use of the writing given her by the young Roman to facilitate her entrance into the hostile camp, and there await an opportunity of reaching the besieged city. Although she fully realized that her life would be more secure among the Romans, or amid the forces of King Agrippa, allies of the former, nevertheless she wished to obey the last commands given her by her father, and to rejoin her friend Sara, and share with her the dangers of the siege.

With eyes blinded by tears she bade a final adieu to the spot where she had so long dwelt, in poverty it is true, but far removed from human perversity; she weepingly kissed the mound which covered the

mortal remains of Simon, and besought the Al
mighty that her days might be few in this valley of
tears. Poor child! in the morning of life she begged
for death and longed for nothing else save a tomb
in the desert!

Unwilling to leave Zabul in that solitude, where,
deprived of food, he would probably resume his
ferocious habits, she decided to take him with her.
Towards daybreak, therefore, she quitted the hut of
Lake Asphaltites, and walking slowly onward, continually turned her head to see the tamarind-tree
which grew over Simon's grave; and when it faded
from her view, she wept inconsolably.

The moment is always painful when we are leaving places wherein our days have passed, if not happily, at least tranquilly; and every step which leads
us among men makes us shudder, since we fear to
be again oppressed by the race of Cain; but the
orphan little dreaded human malignity, because
she was convinced that not even a hair could fall
from her head without the permission of Him who
sees all, and who forgets no one in His infinite
goodness.

The poor girl walked the entire day; and, though
overcome with grief and wearied out with fatigue
and heat, only rested a moment to eat a few dates

and to moisten her lips with some fresh fruit which
she carried with her ; then resumed her journey, and
about sunset came in sight of the Roman encampment.

Since Pompey had rendered Judea tributary to
Rome, the Israelites, weary of being oppressed, had
occasionally but vainly endeavored to throw off the
yoke of the invaders. Their kings, become vassals
not only of the republic, but also of the governors
placed over them by their Roman masters, instead of
taking up the defence of their subjects, urged on by
fear and weakness, made common cause with, or, to
speak more properly, bowed their heads before the
conquerors. Such a state of things lasted many
years, until, under the rule of Gessius Florus, who,
more tyrannical than any of his predecessors, cruelly
oppressed the Jewish people, murmurs began to be
heard throughout the city of Jerusalem ; and in the
month of May in the year 66 of the Christian era,
the twelfth of the reign of Nero, and the seventeenth
of that of Agrippa, King of Judea, the Jews re-
volted and openly took up arms against the Romans.

Vainly did Agrippa strive to calm their exasperated
minds, speaking to the people with sublime eloquence ;
he was driven from Jerusalem, and confined within

3*

the limits of his own little kingdom. However, the rebellion was not unanimous; for many dreaded to fight against those legions which had triumphed over every part of the then known world. The seditious ones were few in number, but rendered strong by desperation, and as is usually the case, forcibly drew along with them their more peaceful countrymen; to the factious were also joined the exiles who, first infesting Judea, had finally introduced themselves into Jerusalem, where they chose as their leader a certain Eleazar, a very daring and at the same time excessively cruel man.

Judea was like a volcano in eruption when Nero sent thither Vespasian as supreme commander of the Roman legions; and the latter associated to himself as lieutenant his son Titus, who, reuniting all the dispersed forces in one body, set out to subdue Galilee.

Flavius Josephus, general of the Hebrews, awaited him with his army; but at the approach of the hostile legions the Jewish soldiers fled precipitately, and the leader sought refuge in Tiberias.

After subduing many rebellious cities, Vespasiar decided to lay siege to Jerusalem; and already th forces scattered throughout Syria had been all collected together, when news reached the camp of

the death of Nero. Then Vespasian suspended hos-
tilities until he should receive fresh orders from
the new Cæsar. It was not long before they learned
that Galba had been proclaimed emperor, and Vespasian sent Titus to Rome to pay his homage at the
feet of their new sovereign.

Galba's rule was short; he died after a seven
months' reign, and was succeeded by Otho, who
being slain within three months of his election, the
German legions proclaimed Vitellius as emperor in
his place. This news reaching the East, the soldiers of Vespasian's army judged that if the Ger-
manic legions had proclaimed their leader Vitellius
as emperor, they could with equal right raise their
chief to the same high dignity; and so they did.
Full of enthusiasm they hailed Vespasian emperor
on the 3d of July in the year 69 of the Christian
era. This election was so generally pleasing that
in a short time all Syria recognized him as Cæsar.

Meanwhile even the Pannonian and Dalmatian
legions declared themselves in favor of Vespasian
and advanced against Vitellius, who vainly strove
to defend himself; but being conquered and forced
to seek refuge in flight, he was torn forcibly from
his hiding place, and cruelly murdered.

Generally recognized as emperor, Vespasian ro-

turned to Rome, leaving to Titus the office of over-
coming the rebellious Israelites, who were more
persistent than ever in their opposition, and, divided
among themselves, were guilty of the most horrible
atrocities. So that in reality the greater part of
the inhabitants of Jerusalem secretly hoped that
the victory of the Romans might put an end to so
much discord and impiety.

Titus wished to subdue the city which alone resisted the Roman eagles; but, naturally of a clem-
ent disposition, he abhorred unnecessary carnage;
and desirous to save the Temple, he waited until
famine should finally open to him the gates of Jerusalem.

The besieging army was composed of four legions,
the same ones which had formerly fought under the
leadership of the valiant Vespasian; in company
with these were the forces of King Solenus and
King Agrippa, who, fighting as allies, were entirely
under the command of the Roman general.

At the time of which we are writing, Titus, wishing to intimidate the rebels, had ordered the tenth
legion to entrench themselves upon Mount Olivet,
which overlooked Jerusalem from the east; and
sending another legion towards Emmaus, he himself encamped with the residue of the army in the

Valley of Saul, thereby to push himself further for
ward and thus to begin the blockade.

It was therefore towards this valley that Anna
directed her steps, hoping that it would be easy for
her to penetrate into Jerusalem ; never reflecting in
her inexperience that it was not so much upon the
besiegers as upon the besieged that the execution of
her design depended.

The sun was near setting when the maiden perceived the Roman tents in the distance, and quickened her steps in order to reach them ere nightfall ;
but overcome by fatigue she seated herself at the
foot of a fragrant acacia, which rose amid a group
of balsam-trees, and watched the sun whose fire-
colored disc was partly hidden behind the Judean
hills.

After resting a few moments she resumed her
journey, and, entirely immersed in her own thoughts,
walked along mechanically, noticing nothing, until
she was startled by a voice which called from a distance in wretched Hebrew :

"Approach no nearer, or I will slay you and
your lion !"

Anna receded, and, recovering from her astonishment, perceived a sentinel on the outskirts of the
camp, who threatened to hurl at her one of those

small murderous iron javelins with which the Roman soldiers assailed the enemy.

The orphan's first impulse was to extend her arms in a supplicating attitude; but the soldier had no intention of wounding her, and the dart was rather directed against Zabul. Anna immediately placed both her hands over the lion's mouth, and making a negative gesture, implying that the lion was not ferocious, advanced towards the soldier; but the latter, ordering her to halt, ran towards her, saying imperiously:

"Do you not know, woman, that it is forbidden, under pain of death, to wander around our camp?"

Anna did not answer, and, trembling with fear, took from her bosom the writing of the young Roman, and handed it to the sentinel, who, unable to read, turned it from side to side, then, losing patience, returned it to the maiden, saying:

"Go away, pretty one, the Roman soldiers are not to be inveigled by the black eyes of the Jewish women!"

With blushing cheeks Anna hastily withdrew from the soldier, and, retracing her steps, re-seated herself at the foot of the acacia-tree. Weakened by fatigue, it would have been impossible to return to the Dead Sea; and, on the other hand, she dared

not remain in that lonely spot exposed to the insults
of the soldiers who might occasionally leave the
tents. Greatly terrified at this thought, she withdrew still further from the Roman camp, and sat
down upon the sand. Shortly after she saw a man
who, walking slowly with his head bent on his
breast, passed before her without seeing her; then
she sprang to her feet, and recognized with some
surprise the stranger who had buried the corpse of
Simon.

Although that man inspired her with terror,
nevertheless Anna hurried up to him, wishing to
ask his advice; but the mysterious individual did
not stop, but, pursuing his way, looked at her sadly,
and extending his hand towards the camp, said to
her, "To-morrow!" Then he passed very near the
sentinel, who apparently never turned his eyes
towards him.

A shudder passed through the maiden's frame at
the thought of that man, whom she had twice before met, but always at baleful moments. She could
not explain to herself why the mere sight of him
caused the blood to freeze in her veins. Fearing to
see him near her, she hid her face in her hands and
then seated herself beside Zabul, her only protector.

Meanwhile night had set in, the stars shone in the

firmament, and the utmost silence reigned around. The evening was beautiful, and sad as the soul of the orphan, who seemed to hear amid that solemn tranquillity the lamenting voice of the prophet who wept over the city full of people, become as a widow, and the princess of provinces made tributary.

The forsaken girl thought lovingly upon her father, now lying in his quiet grave, and saw also in her fancy her childhood's friend; but conquering her sorrow, she looked towards Mount Olivet, where the Man God wept like a man born in this vale of tears. Then she laid her hand upon the lion's shaggy back, and, filled with firm reliance that the Almighty would watch over the daughter of His faithful servant, resigned herself to passing the night lying on the sand of the desert, with no other pillow save the back of the wild beast, no other canopy but the starry vault of heaven, and no protector but God, in whom she placed her entire confidence.

CHAPTER VI.

THE night passed in the Valley of Saul seemed very long to Anna, who about daybreak rose from the ground, where she lay confusedly and undecided; not knowing which course to pursue, she looked towards the Roman camp to see if the sentinel was still at his post. In fact, she perceived a soldier in the distance, and although she felt convinced that he was not the one of the preceding evening, nevertheless she dared not advance, fearing to be driven away a second time.

After some moments' reflection, she resolved to wait until Divine Providence, who always succors those who trust in Him, should open to her a way of entering Jerusalem, and encouraged herself to patience by recalling to mind the words of that mysterious man who had passed near her without stopping.

The sun was shining brilliantly upon the sparkling sand of the valley, when Anna discovered afar several knights who were coming towards her, some mounted on camels and some on horses; and the hope that their leader might prove to be the Roman to whom she had given hospitality, made her heart leap with joy. Standing upright, in order the better to attract notice, she placed herself in front of the lion, who lay dozing with his large head supported on his front paws.

Anna was not mistaken in her hopes; for in a very few moments the young warrior drew in the reins of his Arab steed and stopped near by, to look admiringly at the pretty girl, who, in a natural though picturesque attitude, stood upright beside the crouching beast. He who was born in that city where the master-pieces of Grecian art gave the citizens a taste for everything beautiful, could not fail to be pleased at the sight of that living group, which might have served as a model to Phidias or Praxiteles.

The young man long remained absorbed in his contemplation, but suddenly recognizing the maiden of the Asphaltites, uttered an exclamation of surprise, and springing from his horse ran towards her, saying:

"Perhaps you have come to claim my promise: I thank you for your confidence in me."

Anna's cheeks crimsoned, and lowering her eyes she said, tremblingly:

"I did not come hither to seek a reward for a slight service rendered you, but simply to ask you a favor, which you will not deny 'o the orphan who has no earthly protector."

"Speak!" interrupted the youth, whose face evinced great pity.

"Hear me, I entreat you!" then resumed Anna. "My father on his death-bed ordered me to repair to the house of the only friend who remains to me; she dwells in Jerusalem. Oh! if it be possible to do so, entreat Cæsar's son to grant me a safe conduct into the besieged city."

"Would you enter that den of wild beasts, to fall, perhaps, into the hands of the zealots or the assassins? Are you crazy, maiden?" exclaimed the amazed Roman.

"I must go thither, and I fear nothing," replied Anna, whilst a flash of energetic resolution shone in her black eyes.

The warrior shook his head, remained some moments in silence; then, smiling, added gently:

"If up to this moment you were destitute of friends, henceforward you shall have a powerful one, who will take care of your future. Repair to the Roman camp; before nightfall I also will return thither, and there Titus shall decide your fate."

So saying, the youthful leader turned to one of his suite and spoke to him in a low voice. The latter dismounted from the camel, and drew near the maiden, holding the animal by the reins.

Anna had not the courage to oppose the will of the Roman; the more so that, hoping to soften the heart of Titus by her prayers, she was delighted to enter the camp. Therefore she quietly seated herself upon the back of the camel, and, accompanied by a soldier and by Zabul, took the road towards the Roman encampment.

The camp covered an immense space of ground. In the upper part, upon an artificial eminence, rose the general's tent, and near that were those of the allies and of the Tribunes.

A very wide street separated the upper from the lower part of the camp, and from thence the general-in-chief harangued the troops; there also the punishments were inflicted, excepting that of death, the presence there of the standards and the altars of the gods forbidding it.

The lower part of the camp contained the numerous tents of the soldiery, in the midst of whom the decurias of cavalry were drawn up in two lines.

A noise of many voices echoed around, and everywhere were seen soldiers, part of whom were prac-

tising at *saltus*, to learn to climb the enemy's walls
with agility, or to leap over ditches; part assailed a
stake with blows of a club; and part exercised themselves at *salitio*, that is, in leaping now from one side,
now from another upon a wooden horse, holding a
lance or a sword in their hands. Others, too, showed
their dexterity on horseback, and armed at all points,
rode three times around the camp to accustom themselves to pursue their retreating foes.

Almost all the youths were engaged in warlike
exercises; and the older ones, seated on the ground
before the tents, played at *tessera*,* or at the *ludus
latrun culorum*,† and raising their voices, swore by
all the deities of Olympus.

At the sight of so many fierce-looking soldiers,
who looked at her, smiling insolently, Anna trembled with fear, and would have a thousand times preferred being amidst the most undisciplined Israelites,
than to be wandering among the enemies of her
country.

After a long walk, the soldier who led the camel
ridden by the terrified girl, stopped before a tent
and having entered, came out almost immediately
to desire Anna to follow him.

The maiden timidly descended from the camel,

---

* The tessera had six sides like our dice.　　† Game of chess.

and, following her guide, advanced into the tent, wherein three persons were seated conversing together.

One of these was a young and pretty, though haughty-looking woman, dressed with oriental magnificence, and sitting upon a silken carpet stretched on the ground. At her right sat a man of mature years and imposing aspect, and on her left stood a young man with his arms crossed on his breast, and his head bent in a thoughtful attitude.

The first of these three persons was Bernice; the second, her brother, King Agrippa; and the third, Flavius Josephus.

Flavius was born at Jerusalem. He did not, however, hate the Romans so fiercely as his fellow-citizens; thus he had disapproved of the rebellion more than any one else; but, equally warlike as wise, he had taken up arms to defend his country, and had been chosen commander-in-chief by the insurgent Hebrews. His troops being defeated by Vespasian, he retired into Tiberias, where he continued to fight valorously; then he hurried to relieve Jotapata, which would not have been subdued had not treachery, a plant which springs up in every land and grows vigorously at all seasons, opened the gates to the enemy.

Flavius saved himself with great difficulty by concealing himself in a well, in the bottom of which
was a little door opening into a subterranean, in
which forty of the inhabitants of Jotapata had
taken refuge. At the sight of their general they
resumed.courage, and decided to remain hidden for
some time as they had secured sufficient food to sup
port themselves. But treason tracked the steps of
the valiant Jew. An old woman, who had seen
him lowered into the well, pointed out his hiding-
place to the enraged Romans, who were seeking him
throughout the city. Repairing to the spot indicated, they summoned them to surrender ; but finding
them stubborn in their refusal, they lighted a fire of
straw at the mouth of the well, in order that he and
his companions might all be suffocated by the smoke.
Vainly did Flavius use all his eloquence to induce his
companions to yield, the more so as the Romans did
not impose severe conditions upon them ; they were
immovable, and preferred dying from suffocation
to falling into the hands of their abhorred enemy.
Unable to convince them, Flavius Josephus changed
his tactics ; and since they chose to die, advised them
to kill one another, and thus prevent the Romans
from boasting of their victory. His plan pleased
the poor wretches, who drew lots to decide who of

them should be the first and who the last to die.
Fortune arranged it that Flavius and a young Jew
were the final survivors, and thus, finding no further opposition, they surrendered themselves to the
Romans.

Vespasian experienced great pleasure at the cap-
ture of the Jewish general; and Titus, full of esteem
and sympathy for the learned warrior, exerted himself to save his life; and in order to render his captivity less irksome to him, kept him in the Roman
camp and overwhelmed him with kindness.

When in presence of Bernice, Agrippa, and
Flavius, the daughter of Simon dared not raise her
head, and covered with confusion remained mute.
The rest of the company equally kept silence; at last
Agrippa, advancing towards the maiden, said to her:

" The general has sent you to me, in order that
you should find an asylum under the shade of my
tent.   Therefore, I bid you welcome, as I should
do to any Jewess who might seek King Agrippa's
protection."

Anna, crossing her arms upon her breast, bowed
low in token of gratitude; then was about to speak,
but the king interrupted her to ask:

" What is your name ? "

" Anna, the daughter of Simon," answered the

maiden, without mentioning the illustrious race from which she sprang.

" You come from Jerusalem ; tell me, I pray you, how did you gain permission to pass the gates ?"

" I did not come from Jerusalem, but, on the contrary, from Lake Asphaltites."

" And why did you place yourself in the way of the Roman general ? Perhaps thinking to captivate him by your charms ?"

At these words, which seemed dictated by jealousy, Agrippa's countenance grew livid with anger ; Flavius Josephus smiled, and Anna's cheeks became crimson. Indignation made her knit her brows ; but the humility of the pious girl was stronger than the pain of the insult; therefore, repressing her tears, she added calmly: " I did not seek to meet the general. I resorted to the Roman camp to find some means of entering Jerusalem."

" You seek to enter Jerusalem ? Are you dreaming, maiden ? Possibly you are not aware that many of those who are shut up within its walls would joyfully give ten years of their life to be allowed to quit the city !" exclaimed Agrippa.

" What you tell me, O king, does not discourage me, and I will not abandon my resolution," energetically answered Anna.

4

"Are your father or your brothers fighting within its walls?" asked King Agrippa.

"No; I have no longer a relative upon earth

Flavius Josephus, who had listened with intense interest to the dialogue, drew near the young girl, and after gazing some time admiringly upon her beautiful countenance, said to her:

"But why then should you seek to expose yourself to the hardships and dangers of a siege? Speak, you are in the presence of your king, among your fellow-citizens; and our counsels may guide you better than your own inexperienced judgment."

Anna hesitated and remained silent. Then turning towards Flavius Josephus, who inspired her with more confidence than the rest of the company, resumed: "My wish is to rejoin a friend who was faithful to me in adversity; and should death overtake me in my own country, I shall die in the places sanctified by the word of my Redeemer."

"You are then a follower of the Galilean!" said Agrippa, in contemptuous tones.

Anna bowed her head in token of assent, and Flavius interposed, saying those words which were later to be incorporated in his history of Jewish antiquities, and which the force of truth wrung from the lips of an unbelieving Hebrew:

" If you be a follower of that man * — if he who wrought so many prodigies may be styled a man— the desire which urges you on to die where he died, does not surprise me; and it would seem to me wrong to oppose that course which your faith dic- tates to you."

"It would be wrong to send such a maiden among those men who have become more ferocious than wild beasts," interrupted Agrippa.

" But since she wishes to do so, and if Titus con- sents to it, why should you oppose it, brother?" began Bernice, who longed to see Anna quit the Roman camp as quickly as possible.

Agrippa shook his head and was about to reply, but the sound of brazen trumpets prevented his speaking.

" Titus has already returned!" exclaimed Ber- nice, and rising she hastened to the threshold of the tent. Agrippa and Flavius Josephus followed her, and Anna, remaining behind, saw with considerable astonishment the young Roman whom she had first met on the shores of the Dead Sea, advancing towards the camp at the head of a numerous retinue.

---

* In those days lived Jesus, a wise man, if he can be styled merely a man, for he performed wonderful miracles, and taught the truth to all those who sought to be instructed therein.—Fluv Joseph. Jewish Antiquities B. xviii, cl. 4.

CHAPTER VII.

AGRIPPA, Bernice, and Flavius hastened to meet the Roman general, who, leaping from his horse, entered into conversation with them.

From afar Anna watched the son of Vespasian gesticulate, as if relating some important occurrence, whilst Agrippa's face expressed the utmost surprise; then she saw them all enter the tent of Titus.

Not knowing what course to pursue, the maiden seated herself upon the threshold of the temporary dwelling of Bernice; and more melancholy than usual gave way to sad forebodings, from which, however, she was quickly distracted by the shrill voices of the handmaids of the princess, who roughly ordered her away. Humbled even to tears, she turned her eyes upon the slaves, who possibly, because they were better dressed than herself, considered themselves privileged to ill-treat her, and was about to reprove them for their harshness; but reflecting that to bow the head and suffer in silence the outrages even of an insolent servant, is the painful rule imposed upon the poor, she withdrew in silence, resigning herself to the humiliation, and sat down upon the ground at some distance from the tent— Zabul, as usual, placing himself before her.

Resignation was one of the principal features of Anna's character, and that virtue was not in her case the effect of a weak and apathetic mind, which, unable to do better, takes the world as it comes, and gives to indifference the name of resignation. No, gifted with exquisite sensibility, prouder than most of her sex, she deeply felt humiliation, and the blood of the Asmoneans, boiling within her veins, urged her to rebellion; but the energy of her soul, full of Christian faith, overruled the impetuosity of the perverse passions which lurk within every heart, even the holiest; and at those moments of struggle, forcing her imagination to seek refuge on Calvary, she thought of Him at whose slightest nod the world could be annihilated; but who, resigning Himself to die for our sins, had likewise bowed His head before His oppressors. Seated at some distance from the tent of Bernice, she lowered her eyes every time that the soldiers, passing near her, uttered some unseemly pleasantry. At that torture, for it was a torture to her to be exposed unprotectedly to the mirth of the Romans, the sweat stood upon her forehead, and she with difficulty restrained her tears, until at last, not wishing to see nor hear any thing further, she closed her eyes, and wandered in thought to the abode of the elect, to that happy land where one day her squalid clothing would be changed into splendid garments; where the scoffs and insults of men would no longer cause her to blush, and where reunited to Simon she would bless the Almighty for having condemned her while on this earth to suffer a little ' in order to reward her with the eternal delights of heaven. Her meditation was so profound and so full of sweetness that it might be termed an ecstasy; and she remained many hours thus absorbed, until the voice of warlike trumpets, resounding on all sides, recalled her from that heaven wherein she was mentally wandering, to the stern realities of the Roman camp.

She looked around in dismay, and saw that the entire encampment was in excitement. The tents were hastily lowered, the decurias of cavalry were gathering, camels laden with baggage were passing to and fro, and the infantry, armed at all points, were preparing to set themselves in motion.

Anna supposed that the army was about leaving the Valley of Saul; and in fact she saw it defile along the road which led to Jerusalem.

The general came first at the head of the infantry, then followed the cavalry, and next came the
allied troops and the baggage.   Behind these latter,
escorted by a decuria of cavalry, came Bernice, accompanied by Flavius Josephus, and followed by her
handmaidens, and lastly by a troop of soldiers.

Anna was watching the army with open eyes,
uncertain whether to follow it or to remain where
she was, when Flavius Josephus, quitting Bernice's
side, turned back, and spurring his horse towards
the maiden, said to her :

"Poor child, come with me, since no one cares for
you, as if you were no longer in this world."

Anna followed the Jewish knight, who led her
among the handmaids of the princess, placed her
upon a camel, and then galloped off to rejoin
Agrippa's sister.

The slaves looked with a patronizing air upon
the poor orphan, and many of them derided her.
Anna pretended not to notice it, and gave herself up
anew to her own thoughts, but was soon directed
therefrom by the scream of one of the women, who
at the same time in terror pointed out Zabul to the
soldiers who composed the rear guard.

Anna looked in surprise at the slave, and screamed in her turn at hearing the whizzing of many

arrows which were aimed against her faitl.fu.
friend.

Mortally wounded by the darts of the soldiers,
the lion roared furiously and rushed forward as if to
avenge himself; but a fresh arrow having pierced
him, the poor animal reeled and fell to the ground,
bloody foam issuing from his mouth.

On seeing him prostrate Anna threw herself
from the camel, and ran breathlessly and sobbingly
to kneel beside the beast who had been her faithful
companion in the solitude of the Dead Sea.

Zabul lay with closed eyes, and a smothered rat-
tle issued from his throat. Vainly did Anna call
him; he no longer heard that voice which conquered his native ferocity; at last a shudder passed
over his limbs, he opened his eyes, and expired
looking lovingly on his mistress.

With her head laid upon that of the lion, Anna
paid no heed to the departure of the army; but
continued to weep, when a man passing near her
without stopping, touched her gently on the shoulder, saying:

"Proceed, and do not always weep for the dead!"

Anna immediately recognized the voice; it was
that of the man who had buried her father. Re-
leasing herself from Zabul, she wished to follow

him, but he pointed with an imperious gesture to
wards the army, and then continued his journey on
the road opposite to that followed by the Romans.

Anna stood some moments in indecision, regret-
ting to leave the corpse of the lion unburied; but
reflecting that if she separated herself from the
army, she might perhaps lose all chance of entering
Jerusalem, she extended her arms towards Zabul as
if to bid him a last adieu, and then running like a
gazelle fleeing from the hunters, rejoined Bernice's
handmaidens. Seating herself anew upon the
camel's back, she gave full vent to her grief, without
paying the slightest heed to the taunts of the slaves,
who, to while away the tediousness of the road,
amused themselves by laughing heartily at her ex-
pense.

The army slowly proceeded towards Jerusalem.
That city was about thirty stadium distance from the
Valley of Saul, which formed over an hour's journey,
consequently it soon reached the southern part,
where it halted on the spot called Scopos, having as
a boundary the pool of Betharam, in whose vicinity
many centuries later encamped the Crusaders who
came to free the sepulchre of Christ from the bonds
of the Infidels.

The tents were quickly raised, and Titus estab-
4*

lished a part of the army in the position he judged
fitting for the assault; and whilst the engines of
war were preparing, Anna stood timidly amid a
troop of slaves, who were hurrying to arrange their
lady's habitation, when Flavius Josephus came to
her and called her aside to say to her:

"Are you still firm in your resolution to repair to
Jerusalem?"

"I ask nothing else."

"Very well, follow me. Titus, ever generous,
sends me as a bearer of offers of peace to my fellow-
citizens. I pray fervently that the God of Jacob
may put an end to this war of extermination; but I
have little hopes of it, for the hand of Him who shall
judge among nations shall fill ruins, and shall
crush the heads in the land of many,* weighs
heavily on this city of Sion."

"Divine wrath overtakes us sooner or later,"
replied Anna.

"You may speak thus, maiden, since you are a
follower of Jesus; but come with me, Titus is
opposed to your design, and only Bernice's entreaties have induced him to consent to your accom-
panying me."

Anna's heart bounded with joy, and she cheer-

---

* Psalm cix.

fully followed Flavius, who, after leading her through
a large portion of the camp, ordered her to await
him in a place where three horses were standing in
readiness.

Josephus shortly returned, accompanied by a
young Roman tribune named Nicanor, and having
assisted her to mount the horse destined for her,
they all set cut towards Jerusalem.

The swordsmen used sometimes to walk slowly
along the city walls, pretending to be citizens im-
ploring the aid of the Romans, to draw the enemy
into an ambush. At the sight of two warriors and
a woman riding quietly within reach of their arrows,
they were not slow to understand that they were
sent to open a parley. Possibly they recognized
their former general, whom they soon wrongly supposed to be in league with the Romans; and, contrary to all dictates of generosity, they allowed them
to approach the walls and then treacherously show-
ered down upon them a quantity of arrows.

At the whizzing of the darts Anna's horse reared,
and, uncurbed by her weak and inexperienced
hand, threw her on the ground and fled towards the
camp.

Flavius Josephus, boldly spurring his horse forward, rode even into the midst of the arrows to

speak to his disloyal assailants; vainly, howevei,
for hearing the cries of the Jews joined to the hissing of the darts, he turned and perceived Nicanor,
the inseparable friend of Titus, fall from his horse.
Then springing to the ground he lifted the wounded
man in his arms, and re-mounting his steed, galloped hastily from the spot, without thinking of
Anna, who lay stretched upon the sand.

Left to herself the poor girl gradually lifted her
head, but had not the strength to raise herself from
the ground, her limbs being benumbed by the fall
Feeling her courage deserting her, she closed her
eyes and invoked the Divine assistance. Suddenly
she felt herself lifted carefully from the sand. She
looked up in terror and found herself in the arms
of the mysterious stranger.

Fear having deprived her of strength without di-
vesting her of consciousness, she could see that they
were departing from Jerusalem, and recognized also
in the distance the Roman tents, which rapidly receded from her sight; after that she perceived nothing; but it seemed to her that her conductor
descended into a place whence the light gradually
diminished, and they were soon enveloped in utter
darkness.

Resuming her lost courage, Anna endeavored to

free herself from the arms which encircled her, and demanded imperiously:

"Whither are you taking me?"

"To Jerusalem!" answered a voice which echoed afar in the darkness; then the stranger pressed her hand saying: "Proceed!" and the echoes of the cav ern repeated "Proceed, proceed!"

The hope of finally reaching Jerusalem, caused Anna to forget all her fears; and though convinced that not even a hair of her head could fall unless God so ordered it, she could not however repress a certain shiver at feeling her hand clasped within the icy palm of that mysterious man, whom she now no longer believed to be a supernatural being, since she was certain that he was formed of flesh and blood like herself.

The stranger and the maiden were walking upon an uneven and occasionally stony ground; it was a subterranean passage which led into the besieged city. The girl, the better to reassure herself, tim- idly asked her guide:

"Are you also bound for Jerusalem?"

"Yes," answered the man in a hollow tone, and then added: "The Omnipotent will which directs my steps has suffered me for several days past to wander around the walls without being able to enter within them; now I am forced thither in order to witness the destruction of the Temple, and the extermination of my people."

These fatal words caused Anna to shudder; and not daring to open her mouth, she walked on in silence, mentally invoking the Divine assistance.

After a long ascent, she finally perceived a slight ray of light above her head; but the ground became still more steep, so that the travellers were forced to grope upon their hands and knees. Then the mysterious stranger extended his arms, and with herculean strength raised a stone which covered the entrance into the subterranean, and Anna's heart bounded with joy at the sight of the moon, which cast her silver light even into that dark cavern.

With one bound the unknown reached the street; Anna followed him, and kneeling down in tears kissed the soil of her native city; then she blessed God who had enabled her to fulfil Simon's last wishes.

Having finished her short but fervent prayer, her first thought was to thank the generous man who, saving her from the arrows of the besieged, had guided her into her native city; but he had departed without even stopping for a moment. By the pale light of the moon Anna saw him, like some noc-

turnal phantom, walking slowly behind a group of
old tamarind-trees. Not having courage to follow
him, the poor girl remained motionless, uncertain
what course to pursue, or whither to go at so late an
hour of the night, when none were abroad save the
ferocious zealots who were seeking for corpses, which
they stripped in hopes of finding some money or
some articles of value.

CHAPTER VIII.

LEFT to herselt, Anna looked around to discover where she was, and found that she was standing in the atrium of a ruined house not far from the Hippodrome. The opening out of which she had issued did not seem the egress from a subterranean passage, but rather destined to serve as a drain for water; and even left open as it had been by the mysterious traveller, would have given no cause for suspicion.

The hour was far advanced, and no sound reached her ears save the distant murmur which the night wind wafted along upon its wings.

The besieged, apt at fighting, guarded the walls, ready to defend them from every assault, or garrisoned the numerous towers of Jerusalem. The women, the children, and those unable to bear arms, were barricaded in their dwellings, which they hourly feared to see invaded by the swordsmen, who, quitting their posts, wandered through the city by night and by day committing acts of open robbery and violence.

Anna knew not in what part of the city Sara's house was situated; but remembering that near the pool of Siloam dwelt an aged Christian, who might possibly be able to advise her, turned her steps in that direction.

Jerusalem, which was strengthened by a triple wall and rendered inaccessible by deep valleys, was built upon four eminences, * and surrounded by hills which did not intercept the view of the distant horizon. The Valley of Tyropœon extended to the pool called Siloam, towards which Anna was directing her steps, happy to find herself once more in the city wherein her early days were happily spent; and at that moment she seemed carried back to the time when as a child she ran beside Daniel; but her joy was short-lived; her illusion was dissipated as dust before the wind, as she thought upon her father who had died in exile.

Hastening her steps, as if seeking to fly from her own thoughts, she saw in the distance the boundary wall which she was to pass before reaching the pool, and suddenly stopped in terror at the sight of four soldiers who were running swiftly towards her, clamoring loudly.

Undecided whether to advance or to retreat,

---

* Mount Sion, Mount Moriah, Mount of Olives, Mount Calvary.

Anna remained motionless, nor perceived a warrior who came from the opposite side to that by which the soldiers were approaching.

"I touched her first, and she is mine," cried one of the four, seizing the arm of the maiden, who shrieked for aid ; and in answer to her cries a sonorous voice said in commanding tones :

"Leave that woman in peace, and go your own way!"

Anna's heart beat upon recognizing Daniel's voice, and tremblingly drew nearer him for protection.

"Why do you trouble yourself about her? She shall follow me in spite of you," replied the man who had seized Anna by the arm, as encouraged by the presence of his companions he rushed threateningly towards Daniel.

The young man was not intimidated by their menaces ; and although alone among four, he prepared himself for defence. Pushing Anna backward, he placed himself in front of her, saying resolutely :

"If you want this woman, come now and take her. Villainous wretches! you fly at the sound of the Roman trumpets, and wander about at night in order to oppress the weak."

At this insult the four soldiers furiously attacked Daniel ; but almost immediately the foremost of them threw down his murderous weapon, which he brandished, saying amicably: ﹀

"Forgive me, Daniel! I did not recognize you, nor have I forgotten the day on which I was fighting against the zealots, and you saved my life. Therefore take this night-rover; neither I nor my companions will snatch her from you."

So saying the four soldiers withdrew, laughing over the adventure, and left the young warrior alone with the woman whom he had rescued.

Daniel did not even look at the maiden, and was already about departing, when the latter, taking him by the hand, exclaimed:

"Brother, the daughter of Simon blesses you!"

The young warrior's hand trembled within that of the maiden, and an exclamation of ineffable joy burst from his lips, when by the rays of the moon he recognized Anna's pale face.

For some moments the two young people remained silent, gazing at each other. The impetuosity of their affections was such as to deprive them of speech. At last Daniel, making a strong effort at self-control, asked in a faltering voice:

"You here, Anna? but whence do you come, and why do you wander alone at this hour? I thought you still by the shores of the Dead Sea."

"The mortal remains of Simon sleep beneath the sands of the desert, and I have come hither to rejoin Sara."

"Imprudent girl!" said the young warrior, while a sad expression passed over his speaking countenance.

"Why do you call me imprudent? Do you not remember that by the shores of the Lake Asphaltites you implored me to follow you to Jerusalem?"

"I did not then suppose that the city of David would become worse than Nineveh, and that the chosen people would stain themselves by such enormous crimes."

Anna, not knowing what answer to make to Daniel's remark, began relating to him the means by which she had been enabled to enter Jerusalem; and Daniel, unable to imagine who her mysterious protector might be, resolved to close the entrance to the subterranean passage, lest it might be used by the enemy.

Anna and her lover walked on in silence, one beside the other, and the daughter of Simor spoke not, fearing to encourage Daniel to converse upon a sentiment which she wished at every cost to see eradicated from his heart. At last a deep sigh escaped his lips, and in accents harmonous as those of an eolian harp, he murmured the name of Anna.

The maiden bowed her head upon her breast, and feigned not to hear that voice which touched the most hidden fibres of her heart; and the youth continued sadly :

" Anna, I should rejoice to know you were far from here. Hitherto I have fought valiantly in defence of the Temple, but henceforth, knowing you to be exposed to the wiles of thieves who profane all that you hold most dear, I shall turn my back to the enemy in order to rush to your assistance."

" You will not close your ears to the voice of honor," replied the maiden ; and shaking her head, she added : " You are valiant, Daniel, but your prowess will not save our country. Jerusalem is condemned to expiate the blood of the Son of God."

Daniel kept silence; the young girl's words responded to a voice which was ever resounding in the depths of his heart.

The two young people walked through the most unfrequented streets, for Daniel purposely lengthened the road which would lead them to Sara's house, in order to avoid exposing the young girl to the gaze of the swordsmen. Although he was ready to defend her at the cost of his life, nevertheless he did

not wish to fall in vain, since he might be overcome by the number of his assailants, and thus
leave the maiden deprived of protection. Such a
thought made him shudder, and he, so daring and
courageous, moved onward, gazing fearfully around
him.

The streets which they traversed were deserted;
here and there were some few houses which had
been burned or destroyed by the seditious party, in
the delusive hope of finding some hidden treasures.
Everything told of the ruin, squalor, and desolation
caused by war; naught was wanting save the voice
of the prophet Jeremiah to lament over its misery.

Suddenly Anna shuddered at the sight of a number of corpses lying on the ground along the street,
which, festering under the burning sun of a summer's
day, poisoned the air with their insupportable miasma. Seizing Daniel's arm she closed her eyes and
asked in terror:

"Who are these?"

"They are the victims of the intestine war which
decimates the Jewish nation," answered Daniel.
"They are those unfortunate wretches who, thought to
be friendly to the Romans, were surrendered by the
followers of Eleazar, son of Simon, or by those of
John of Giscala, who have now sought safety with-

in the walls of the Temple.* Woe to those who venture to give burial to the fetid remains : either the zealots or the swordsmen would immediately murder them."

" Let us quicken our pace," said Anna, running hastily onwards to escape the horrible scene; but after a few more steps she drew back in terror at the sight of a fearfully mutilated corpse.

" Another victim," said Daniel, sadly ; then added, " That shapeless corpse upon which you were so . nearly treading, sheltered the soul of a truly virtuous and venerated man. Thinking him to be wealthy, the most ferocious of the zealots rushed to his house to plunder it; but finding nothing therein, declared that he must have swallowed his gold, and forthwith ripped open his stomach." †

---

* The faction of the zealots, fearing to have merited the anger of the people, took refuge in the Temple.

† The Romans themselves were guilty of similar barbarities. Here are the words of the modern and erudite historian of Jerusalem: " Some of the fugitives, thinking for the future, sold their most precious effects, and melting down the gold, swallowed it, fearing the thieves. Upon reaching the Roman camp, they examined their excrements in search of the gold which they had received into their stomachs. One of these avaricious misers was seen by Arabs and Syrians in the act of recovering his treasure. The news quickly spread over the camp. This discovery so excited the cupidity of the soldiery, that not only the Arabs and Syrians, but even some of the Romans, supposing that all the Hebrews, previous to abandoning Jerusalem, had swallowed quantities of the precious metal, placed themselves in ambush, and whenever they could lay their hands upon them did so, and many they disemboweled alive."—*Hist. of Jerusalem*, by F. Cassin da Perinaldo, Vol. 1, page 409.

"And yet you fight for such monsters of cru
elty!" exclaimed the maiden.

"I fight for the Temple, beside those few valorous sons of Israel who, weary of bowing their
necks beneath the yoke of the idolaters, rebelled
against Rome, and now hungry and half naked,
they defend their country like true lions of Judea,
baring their breasts to the enemy's arrows."

As he spoke, the eyes of the valiant Jew shone
with warlike enthusiasm, and he raised his noble
head with a martial air.

After many tortuous windings the two young
people reached the house built by Pontius Pilate
on the spot whence the Son of God had been
dragged like a malefactor, in order to prove to
those redeemed by His blood, that even a God
could be trampled upon and vilified by human perversity.

That spot was sacred for Anna; quitting Daniel's side she kneeled down to kiss the ground; and
on rising heard the murmur of many distant voices
which were echoed even where she stood.

"Who shouts thus?" anxiously asked the maiden.

"It is the cry which calls the combatants to the
walls," answered the young warrior.

"Go where honor calls you," resumed Anna.

"Still a few more steps and we reach Sara's dwelling," replied Daniel.

The cries became louder, and Anna perceived that Daniel's heart was struggling between the desire of fighting and that of protecting her ; and fearing that he might be punished if found wanting in his duty, said to him beseechingly :

"Go, I implore you. Point out to me Sara's house, and I will run thither; but oh! do not expose yourself to death unnecessarily, and contrive to let me see you to-morrow."

Daniel sighed and withdrew in obedience to the request of the maiden, who, prostrating herself before the pretorium of Pilate, exclaimed :

"Son of God, grant that thy blood may not have been shed vainly in behalf of Daniel; save him from death in order that he may die a Christian ! "

Rising from the ground, the young girl pursued her way, but stopped hastily at the sound of many voices which seemed approaching the spot where she stood. Fearing to encounter a horde of robbers she looked around to see where she might conceal herself, and perceiving the pillar of a ruined house, hid herself behind it.

Shortly after a troop of zealots passed in front of her, but no one discovered her. When she heard no

5

more, she issued from her hiding-place and walked onward, and with renewed courage started once more on her journey, but stumbled over a bundle of clothes lying upon the ground. Impelled by curiosity she opened it, and found it contained the dress of a man. A thought flashed across her mind : masculine attire might protect her from robbers. She forthwith retired behind the pillar, and put on the clothes, rolling up her own and placing them under her arm ; then she proceeded along the road indicated by Daniel, and soon reached a narrow street bordered on both sides by wretched houses.

The ground was stony and covered with filth, and exhaled a pestilential miasma ; and Anna, groping through the darkness, scarcely distinguished the objects around her, for the moon did not shed her rays upon that squalid road.

Halting before a house of better aspect than the rest, she stood for some moments in doubt ; then knocked gently at the wooden posts of a badly-closed door, and listened, fearing that it would not be opened by reason of the lateness of the hour, for it was long past midnight ; but in a few moments she saw a faint glimmer through the portals, then the door opened, and a woman seizing her hand, said :

" Already returned, dearest husband ? "

"Sara, it is I," exclaimed the maiden, tenderly embracing the friend who had been faithful to her in misfortune.

Sara withdrew herself from her encircling arms, and taking up a lamp which she had placed upon the ground, threw its light upon the young girl's face, then exclaimed joyfully:

"Anna, my dear sister!"

"Yes, it is I, an orphan and unprotected, who come to beg an asylum."

"Poverty seeks aid from poverty!" said the woman, sadly; then added: "Follow me, sister, and as long as there is one bushel of wheat remaining to the wife of Joel, she will divide it with the poor."

So saying Sara tenderly pressed her friend's hand, and carefully closing the door, led her into her poor but hospitable habitation.

CHAPTER IX.

SARA's dwelling consisted only of one ground floor, with the roof in the form of a terrace, and according to the Mosaic law * surrounded by a low wall. It contained but few rooms; into one of which, somewhat larger than the others, whose stone walls were coarsely cemented together, Sara led the young stranger.

The room contained only the strictest necessaries, namely, two benches, a wooden table, and a straw mattress.

Seated upon the floor, her head leaning against one of the stone benches, was a woman, whose long hair hung dishevelled upon her shoulders, and her face, though pale and meagre, retained traces of beauty destroyed by intense sufferings. Her eyes were closed, and she seemed troubled by frightful dreams, and on her knees lay an infant of a few months wrapped in filthy rags.

---

* " When thou buildest a new house, thou shalt make a battlement to the roof round about."—*Deuteronomy* xxii. 8.

Anna paid no attention to the sleeper, but fixed her loving eyes upon Sara, whom she had not seen for many months.

Sara was a beautiful woman of about twenty-two years of age, tall and exceedingly graceful in figure. Her lovely features were rather of the Grecian than the Jewish type, and their expression changed every moment, according to the emotions which filled her sensitive and impassioned heart.

For some seconds the two friends looked at each other in silence ; then Sara, knitting her eye-brows, said in gently reproving tones :

" Why are you dressed in men's clothes ? Do you not know that it is forbidden by the law ? " *

" Your law does not regulate my actions," replied Anna ; then she related how she had found the clothes, and told also of Simon's death, of the way in which she had reached Jerusalem, and ended her narration by asking : " Where are your children, Sara ? I do not see them."

At this question, Sara grew deadly pale, her eyes filled with tears, and sighing deeply, she began in a voice broken by sobs :

" Jonathan alone remains to me . . . Hagar, my daughter with the blue eyes and curly hair, died a

---

* The Mosaic law prohibited women from wearing the clothes of a man

few days since, only one year old. My milk, poisoned by my continual anxiety for the life of Joel, killed her . . . poor darling! She was so pretty when she stretched out her little arms towards me, smiling like a little angel . . . Here is all that is left me belonging to her."

And taking a curl from her bosom, Sara covered it with tears and kisses.

"Be calm, dear friend, do not murmur against the divine will," said Anna, pressing the hand of the poor mother, who, drying her tears, continued:

"I ought not to weep for Hagar, who died ere experiencing the hardships of life, since Jonathan remains to become the support and comfort of my old age, as well as that of Joel, who will outlive me. Yes, Joel will outlive me," she said, in that excited voice which showed the strength of the wife and mother's love. "My husband is as valiant as Maccabeus, and God will watch over him. You cannot understand, Anna, how dear Joel is to me. I love him with the love of a wife, a mother, and a sister combined. When I wept over my child's death, he said to me: 'Weep not, Sara!' and my tears ceased at the mere sound of his voice."

The impassioned accents of Joel's wife inspired

Anna with pity, as she thought that at any moment her unfortunate friend might become a widow.

"It is some time since you have seen my son; come with me and behold him asleep."

So saying, Sara led her friend into an adjoining room, where upon a low couch lay a boy of three years of age, with his arms stretched by his sides, and his brow covered with curly brown hair.

The mother approached the bed holding a lamp in her right hand, and shading the light with her left, so that its rays should not fall upon the child's face; then smiled, and said, with maternal pride:

"Look at him, Anna, and tell me if you ever saw so beautiful a child?"

Anna bent forward to see the infant, who tossed his arms in his sleep and smilingly murmured a name.

"He is calling his father," said Sara; then she placed the lamp on the ground, and leaning her head against that of her child, inhaled the breath which issued from his mouth.

Anna admired the lovely group formed by the mother and child, and thought to herself that maternal love is a great joy even amid the greatest trials of life.

At last Sara motioned Anna to follow her; and

stepping gently, entered the adjoining room, where on hearing a groan from the woman who was sleeping with her head leaning against the stone bench, the maiden asked her:

" Who is that ? "

" Her name is Maria," replied Sara ; "the wife of a wealthy man, born on the opposite shore of the Jordan. She came with him to Jerusalem to celebrate the Passover. The siege prevented their returning home, and the poor creature took refuge in a house situated near Herod's palace. There her son was born. The zealots, knowing her to be wealthy, invaded her dwelling, and after robbing her, murdered her husband. The poor widow, crazed by sorrow, concealed herself in a subterranean, carrying with her the little money she had succeeded in saving from the cupidity of the zealots ; but even there they pursued her ; and the wretches robbed her of her last obolus, and even of the clothes in which she had wrapped her child, and would have killed her, had not Joel, at the head of the party who hate the zealots, flown to her assistance. We, although poor—for all our possessions are in Jericho—offered her an asylum in our house. Her mind is entirely gone, and constantly tormented by frightful visions, she will never lie down but always sleeps in a sitting posture, in spite of all my entreaties."

"Poor creature!" cried Anna, wiping away the tears which pity drew from her eyes.

Maria seemed in a troubled sleep. She trembled nervously, and breathed with difficulty, as if oppressed with nightmare; but suddenly waking on hearing the feeble and pitiful moaning of her child, she hastily brushed away the dishevelled hair from her forehead, and seizing the infant, strained him to her bosom to give it nourishment.

The miserable little creature eagerly sucked his mother's empty breast, but, unable to extract there from the smallest drop of milk, writhed his hands and feet, crying piteously.

"He is hungry," said Maria; and in those simple words was such an expression of agony, that they seemed almost a curse; then rising, she placed the baby on the floor, exclaiming: "Die, then, since your mother's exhausted bosom denies you your natural food!"

So saying, with distended eyes, she bent threateningly over the child; but at the moment Sara ran towards her, and pushing her away, took the infant in her arms, saying:

"Why did you not tell me that your milk was

5*

dried up? Even were Hagar still alive, as I share my bread with you, so would I have divided my child's nourishment with your baby."

"It is only since yesterday that he has suffered hunger," replied Maria, whilst Sara caressed the infant; then she watched the kind woman with grim looks as if she were jealous of her.

Anna, guessing the cause of the poor mother's jealousy, feared that she might become delirious, therefore said to her gently:

"Come with me and leave Sara to nurse your child."

"Who are you?" asked Maria, looking wonderingly at her.

"My name is Anna, the daughter of Simon."

"She is a friend of mine, who only arrived in Jerusalem yesterday," said Sara.

"If you only arrived yesterday, maiden, depart hence as quickly as possible, if you would not fall into the hands of the execrable men who defend Sion—into the hands of those wretches who, by their abominations, provoke the divine wrath. Depart ere the sins of the Jewish nation render this city a desert over which salt shall be sown, and where the bewildered traveller, reaching the city of David, shall ask if it really stood here!"

Anna and Sara vainly strove to calm the excited Maria, who with her arms extended in anger, and with fierce looks, inspired them with terror; then Joel's wife, wearied with watching, resolved to retire, and although it was near daybreak, begged Anna to follow her example; but scarcely had the two women laid themselves down to rest, when knocks were heard at the door of the house.

"It is Joel," cried Sara, trembling with joy as she ran to open the door; and returned with her hand resting upon the shoulder of a young man, whom Anna immediately recognized as her husband. The mother ran joyfully to her boy's couch and woke him, saying:

"My son, my son, your father has returned."

The boy awoke, looked about him with a bewildered air, and recognizing his father, held out his arms towards him, screaming with delight.

After Joel had kissed his son several times, calling him by various tender names, Anna approached him, saying smilingly:

» "Well met, brother!"

"Daniel spoke to me about you," answered Joel, pressing the maiden's hand.

"Daniel!" exclaimed Anna, blushing.

"Yes, he generously yielded me the hour of

liberty which was allowed to him. I could not leave the walls; but the desire of seeing my wife and child tormented me, for the kisses of my dear ones enable me to forget the carnage and profligacy which contaminates my country. Therefore Daniel, generously sacrificing himself for me, seat me in his place. I own I was rather selfish, but he is neither a husband nor a father."

"But he is however a lover," said Sara, looking pityingly at the maiden, as if asking her forgiveness for Joel's innocent selfishness.

"Joel is right; Daniel has neither a wife nor a child to watch for him, and, excepting friendship, no other feeling should lead him to this house," answered the maiden, whose love for the friend of her childhood was a poor affection nourished by holy hopes, sacrifices, and sadness.

The spouses remained for some time in silence, then Sara made Joel seat himself upon Jonathan's little couch, and sitting beside him, asked him if the Romans had yet begun the assault.

"They began it yesterday," replied Joel. "Simon of Giora, who has been defending the walls with us, besought John of Giscala to quit the Temple, to lay aside the old causes of discord, and to unite his forces with those which were defending Jerusalem.

Meanwhile, we with the balistæ * taken from the
Romans before the arrival of Titus, defend the walls,
but the enemy give us no respite, but throw the
largest stones against us from their engines of war;
but our outposts see them from afar, and in accord-
ance with the orders given, cry *Barba;* † at that
word we, all stretching ourselves on the ground, hear
the whistle of the stones, which pass over our heads.
Vainly do the Romans color them brown; we see
them all the same, and very few of the Jews have
so far been wounded. The enraged enemy shower
darts upon us, but we in our turn are not idle; for
while the former are fighting to conquer Jerusalem,
we fight for the defence of the Temple, of our wives,
and of our children; and each one of us knows that,
if conquered, slavery awaits him; and we fight like
furious lions, eagerly seeking death or victory. To-
night one of the wooden towers built by the enemy
crumbled,‡ and the Romans, greatly intimidated,

---

* Engines to cast stones, taken when Cestius Gallus was forced to retreat.

† "They placed in the towers sentinels, charged to keep their eyes always
fixed upon the enemy's engines, and to give the alarm whenever they were
seen to move, which they did by uttering the Hebrew word *Barba*, which
signifies *the son cometh;* that is, the stone comes issuing from the mouth
of the warlike machine. At the pre-arranged signal, all the Jews who were
on the walls extended themselves upon the ground."—*Hist. of Jerusalem*, by
F. Cassini da Perinaldo, Vol. I., p. 385.

‡ "Three towers were constructed by order of Titus, destined to drive the
besieged from the walls. One of them fell to pieces during the night. At
the noise the Romans ran to arms, in great trepidation, not knowing what
had happened."—*Flavius Josephus' "Jewish Antiquities."*

abandoned the assault and sought refuge within their camp, whither our arrows contrived to reach them; but to-morrow, when the sun rises over the Judean mountains, they will return to assail us. This exterminating and obstinate war must soon terminate, but perhaps it will end with our deaths and the destruction of our Temple; a fatal presentiment tells me so, and I have little or no hope."

" Oh, cease ! " exclaimed Sara, who at the thought that her husband must return to the walls, burst into agonizing sobs.

" Weep not, Sara ! " resumed Joel, " weep not ! Should I die in the fight, you at least will survive; you will live for Jonathan, and will be faithful to my memory."

" Cease Joel, do not speak to me of death. Have you forgotten that on the day on which I became your wife, I swore that the same tomb should receive our remains? If you die in the fight I will die with you; for life without you would be a slow martyrdom."

" And our boy ? "

" Anna will be a mother to him; but you will not die. The chosen people will repulse the idolatrous invaders, and Jerusalem shall once more be free and victorious."

" Jerusalem shall fall. God said of its inhabitants: 'There shall be sent upon them a nation from afar, whose tongue they cannot understand, a most insolent nation, that will show no regard to the ancient nor have pity on the infant, and their carcasses shall be meat for the fowls of the air and the beasts of the earth, and there shall be none to drive them away!'" * exclaimed a sonorous voice behind Joel's shoulder.

Joel turned in surprise and beheld Maria, who, with her long hair hanging dishevelled over her shoulders, her vacant look, and her emaciated child pressed closely to her bosom, stood on the threshold of the door, an object of pity.

Although Sara was accustomed to the sight of the poor woman, yet she could not help experiencing a secret terror, and clung fast to her husband, hiding her face in his bosom.

Taking the hand of the demented creature and drawing her with her, Anna left the two young spouses to console each other, whilst they caressed their child, who was too young either to understand his mother's anguish, or ·to admire the courage and energy of his father.

Joel remained more than an hour at his home, but

* Denteronomy xxviii. 49, 50.

finally forcibly released himself from his child's em-
braces and after recommending him to Anna's care,
returned to his place of duty, leaving the maiden in
charge of two women, one of whom had partly lost
her mind through grief, and the other was about to
lose her reason entirely.

Looking at Sara, who wept bitterly over Joel's departure, and hearing Maria singing listlessly to her
child, Anna turned her eyes towards heaven, saying
sadly:

"When on your death-bed, dearest father, you desired me to repair to Jerusalem, possibly you fore-
saw that your daughter would be able to perform
some work of mercy in that city."

Then she seated herself at Sara's feet, and with
her sweet voice and persuasive eloquence, restored
her friend's courage and led her to hope that Joel
would not fall a victim to the cruel and exterminating war which was then raging so fiercely around
them.

CHAPTER X.

WHILST Joel and Daniel were fighting upon the walls of Jerusalem, Anna dwelt in Sara's house, and was an angel of goodness towards the two poor mothers; occupying herself in domestic labors, taking care of Maria's infant, who no longer found nourishment in Sara's bosom, and amusing Jonathan in order to prevent his complaints from worrying his wretched mother, who paid no attention to things around her, but being constantly possessed by the idea that Joel would fall a victim, wept unremittingly. Not even Jonathan's tender caresses would diminish her sorrow, for the child's pretty face reminded her of the only man she had ever loved, who would perhaps precede her into the tomb, leaving her a disconsolate widow.

Maria was less sad than Sara, for she had no husband to fear for, and seeing her son grow stronger daily, her mind had frequent lucid intervals wherein she for the time being regained all her reason.

Encouraging her two friends, both by word and

example, Anna inspired others with hopes which were far from her own heart; for she was convinced that, sooner or later, Jerusalem would fall into the hands of the Romans. And truly she was not deceived, for the condition of the guilty and wretched inhabitants became worse daily.

Notwithstanding the desperate defence of the Jews, the Romans remained masters of the two outer walls. There was no more to be gained but the third circlet. Yet Titus, generous-hearted by nature and a great admirer of the beautiful, did not wish to destroy the Temple, whose imposing magnificence far exceeded that of any Roman edifice. Nor did he desire to carry on unnecessary carnage, hoping that the besieged, weary of fighting, and finding themselves deprived of all aid, would surrender at discretion.

However, he decided to make a final attempt, trusting to terrify the enemy by showing them the strength and excellent condition of his army; therefore for three consecutive days he made a review of his legions, furnishing them with abundance of food, within the enclosures of which he had suc ceeded in gaining possession.

From both towers and walls the Jews watched the spectacle, which to them was like the punish-

ment of Tantalus; and at the sight of the battering-
rams, the catapults, and the balistæ, drawn out in
battle array, they shuddered at the thought of the
power and strength of the enemy, to whom they,
the besieged, had nothing to oppose save a few
machines of war, the inner wall of a city already
half conquered, and the desperate courage of those
who were fighting for their own country.

The trial proving ineffectual, and the obstinacy
of the Jews increasing, the irritated Roman general
gave orders that they should at once begin the
attack of the inner enclosure; but Flavius Josephus
pleaded for his fellow-citizens, and whilst the Romans were raising the platforms on which to plant
their engines of war, he repaired to the second enclosure, and mounting the wall, harangued his brethren, urging them to surrender to those who ruled
the world by conquering every part of it. At the
same time he vaunted the clemency of Titus; but
his words were vain, and in fact still further exasperated the Jews, who, reaching the climax of their
anger, heaped imprecations upon their former leader,
cursing even the mother who had conceived him,
and the day wherein he had been born; then, to add
to their insults, they aimed a shower of arrows
against him, which, putting an end to his eloquence,

took from him all hope of persuading the inhabitants of Jerusalem to surrender.

But there were not a few among the besieged,
who, convinced by the arguments of Flavius, and
seeing their own extermination at hand, sought to
elude the watchfulness of their associates, and escaping from the walls, took refuge in the Roman camp.
Here they were generously welcomed by Titus, and
obtained permission to go whither they pleased,
upon condition of never more bearing arms against
the Romans.

Those, too, who could not succeed in escaping,
found out another expedient, namely, they mingled
among the soldiers who issued forth from the walls
to attack the Romans who were preparing the
ground to plant their battering-rams, and falling
intentionally into the hands of the enemy, begged
that their lives might be spared.

The prisoners daily increasing, Titus saw himself
under the sad necessity of appearing very cruel,
being unable to keep them all, since their number
was far superior to that of his entire army; nor
could he set them at liberty without great impru
dence, as he might thereby provide himself with an
enemy who might annoy him in the rear whilst he
was besieging Jerusalem.

Forgetting his usual clemency, the Roman general, adopting a course, necessary certainly, but which might have been less cruel, ordered that many of the captives should be crucified; and, according to the Jewish historian, the number of the condemned was so great that the space was insufficient for the crosses.

This cruel deed greatly irritated the defenders of Jerusalem, who cried out, pointing to the crucified: " Behold the fate reserved for us by the Romans! Let us therefore die in defence of the Temple."

This being repeated to Titus, he sent many of those who had found refuge within his camp to Jerusalem, bidding them inform the Jews that only those prisoners who had frequently abused his confidence had been crucified; but that those who had voluntarily surrendered themselves, had found him a generous enemy.

Meanwhile the Romans gave a moment of respite to the besieged, who, by order of John of Giscala, dug a trench in the vicinity of the tower of Antonia, *Ferris Antonia,* * by means of which they might secretly make their way under the enemy's

---

* A fortress of Jerusalem, founded by Hyrcanus, and enlarged and strengthened by Herod, who called it Antonia in honor of Mark Antony It stood on a high and precipitous rock, at the northwest angle of the Temple.— *Translator*.

engines of war.   Daniel and Joel were standing together, somewhat apart from the soldiers, immersed
in their own sad thoughts.

Daniel, pale and melancholy, was looking fixedly
upon the crosses which rose within view of Calvary,
as if Titus wished to avenge the death of the Redeemer upon the sons of those who had demanded
his crucifixion ;   and Joel had turned his eyes towards Jericho, then illuminated by the rays of the
rising sun.

"Of what are you thinking?" said Joel, inter
rupting his friend's meditations.

"I am thinking that Jerusalem will fall, notwithstanding our efforts, and that should we not die in
the fray, we shall be suspended upon a cross, like
our brethren."

"I quite agree with you," answered Joel, sighing ;
and the former added :

"I shall die with my country, and shall die joyfully, for no tie binds me to the earth, and, save you,
no one will mourn my loss."

"And Anna? you forget her whom you so
greatly love, and who fully returns your affection."

"That love was a dream.   I fancied myself
beloved, but deceived myself; that maiden's cold
heart never beat for me.   She has forbidden me to

visit your house, although she kLows that at any moment I may fall in battle."

"You are mistaken, and greatly misjudge that pure-hearted child, who, under her apparent coldness, bears a warm heart. Believe me, it is faith alone which separates you from her, and without that barrier which divides you, you would long since have been her spouse."

"Cease! do not speak to me of her who no longer loves me!" replied Daniel, turning aside his head to conceal a tear which belied his words.

"If you no longer love her, death will be more welcome to you than to me, whom it will eternally separate from an adored wife," said Joel ; and look·ing towards Jericho, he added, pointing to the distant mountains :   •

"I had thought to pass many long and happy years thither, beside the only woman whom I ever loved, and hoped to go down to the grave in a green old age, surrounded by my numerous descendants. But it was merely a dream, which vanished rapidly, as vanish all human hopes here below."

"Listen to me, Joel, and follow the advice of a true friend. You have done much for your country , aud did her salvation depend upon your life, I would say to you: Shed even the last drop of your blood. But neither your valor nor your death will hinder her fall. Titus is generous towards those who trust in him; repair to the Roman camp with your wife, your child, and with Anna, and when the city of David no longer exists, you will live happily elsewhere."

"Friend," said Joel, in a faltering voice, "your affection for me leads you to give counsel which you would not follow. I am grateful to you for it, but I will not lay down my arms, neither will I ask pardon from a Roman. I dearly love my spouse, but I should prefer that death should forever separate me from her, rather than to read contempt in her looks; for death is far preferable to the scorn of one whom we love, and Sara would despise me could I commit so vile an action."

"Who better than yourself merits a long and happy life?" exclaimed Daniel, pressing his friend's hand, while the latter added:

"I do not deserve it; and if I must die, I desire naught else save to die with my head pillowed upon the lap of my beloved wife."

Scarcely had Joel uttered these words, when an arrow, shot at random from the enemy's camp, struck him on the right breast, wounding him mortally.

Daniel uttered a groan, and seeing his friend reel,

extended his arms to support him, then laying him gently on the ground, and taking the arrow from the wound, shuddered to witness the torrent of blood which gushed therefrom.

Extended on the ground, with eyes closed and pallid features, Joel murmured Sara's name, wishing to die with that loved word upon his lips.

Daniel stood petrified with grief; he had frequently seen death strike down his companions-in-arms, but until that day no one dear to him had fallen beside him. Now his usual energy disappeared before the sorrow he experienced at the sight of his dying friend, and he watched him with indescribable anxiety, as if striving to count his last gasps. Finally he aroused himself; a thought had entered his mind; he, remembering that amid the zealots who defended the Fortress Antonia was one who by means of a balsam composed of aromatic herbs had saved many of the wounded, left Joel to run in search of him, and quickly returned, accompanied by a vulgar and ferocious-looking man, who glanced with indifference upon the wounded man, and then leaned over him to examine the injured breast.

A shudder, caused by pain, shook Joel's body. He opened his eyes and asked in a faint voice :

6

"Is my wound mortal?"

"It is severe, though not mortal, and my balsam can cure it," replied the zealot.

"Dearest Sara, I may yet see you once more!" said Joel, and then added with some difficulty: "Enable me once more to take up arms in defence of my country, and my eternal gratitude shall be yours."

"Gratitude!" began the zealot, shrugging his shoulders with a contemptuous gesture. "Gratitude!" he repeated, whilst a flash of Jewish avarice passed over his countenance. "If you wish me to heal you, you must offer me another reward."

"I possess nothing," sadly answered the sufferer.

"So much the worse for you, as in that case I have nothing to give you," said the wretch, turning his back upon the dying man; but at the same moment, Daniel, who had with difficulty restrained his anger during the previous dialogue, seized him by the throat, saying threateningly:

"And you, cursed son of Belial, what will you give in exchange for your life?"

The zealot struggled furiously to release himself from that grasp, but in vain, for the muscular hand of the young warrior encircled his throat as with an iron collar, and finding himself half strangled, he stammered supplicatingly:

"Let me go free ... and I will save your wounded friend."

Daniel, not trusting the words of the zealot, took his sword from him; then standing beside him with a menacing air, added :

" Take care of my friend, and, remember, should he die through your wickedness, you shall not survive him one instant, and I know how to reach you, even should you hide within the bowels of the earth."

"Fear nothing; I have no wish to be strangled," answered the zealot, breathing more freely, and looking loweringly at the young warrior. Then taking from the pocket of his doublet a phial of balsam, he let fall a few drops upon the wound, and binding it up as best he might, was about taking up the phial which he had placed on the ground and retiring; but Daniel, staying his arm, took possession of the phial himself, and then followed him to say impressively :

"I know you, and am aware that you would be quite capable of substituting a poison. Therefore depart, I will myself take charge of Joel ; and never more come near me, if you would not be separated soul from body."

The zealot answered not, but withdrew, making a threatening gesture, indicative of an intention to revenge himself.   Fortunately Daniel did not see it, for aided by a soldier, who was just passing at that moment, he had raised Joel from the ground to conceal him behind a little hillock of sand, where he would be protected from the shafts of the enemy; and as he was tenderly placing him in a reclining posture, he said to him :

"Would you like to be taken home? Speak, and I will carry you thither in my arms."

"I should die before reaching there," answered Joel; and then gasping for breath, he added: "This evening seek out Sara .... Tell her to come here to render my death agony less painful."

A tear rolled down Daniel's cheek as he leaned down to comfort his wounded comrade; but hearing just then the noise of a fragment of rock thrown by the Roman battering-ram, and the voices of his companions-in-arms shouting: *To the walls, to the walls !* he stood some moments in great hesitation; for although he did not like to leave his dying friend, it seemed more his duty to return to his place among the combatants.   He thought of his threatened country conquered ; and giving a farewell kiss to poor Joel, and recommending him to the care of the above-mentioned soldier, he ran hastily towards the spot where the battle raged the most furiously.

CHAPTER XI.

DANIEL intended rushing into the thickest of the fight; but informed by a soldier that John of Giscala wished to see him, he immediately turned his steps towards the headquarters of that chief of the zealots, who then shared the supreme command with Simon of Giora. Daniel had soon a difficult enterprise on hand; for he received orders to introduce himself with a few soldiers into the subterranean way which led under the Roman works, and to set fire to a mine already prepared there.

It was extremely dangerous to carry out such an order; but the heart of the valiant warrior never faltered; and with cool courage and still greater prudence than is usually found in so young an officer, he began the difficult task.

Advancing into the excavation, the roof of which was supported by wooden beams, he carried thither logs covered with bitumen, and set fire to them exactly at the moment they had arrived directly under the enemy's works.*

* " Jewish Antiquities," vol. iii., p. 416.

In a flash the fire cons.med the beams, and the excavated ground fell in, carrying with it the breastworks, and a cloud of smoke mingled with the dust of crumbling walls rose towards heaven.

Not a few of the Romans perished in the explosion; and the survivors, stricken with terror, fled in confusion towards the camp. There the reproofs and eloquence of Titus alone succeeded in re-assuring them, and inducing them to shake off their fear that the very ground on which they stood would crumble under their feet.

Daniel having brought the enterprise to a successful termination, immediately quitted his companions-in-arms, who overwhelmed him with praises, and hurried to the spot where Joel lay; and covered with dust, stained with bitumen, and bathed in sweat, he kneeled beside the wounded man, saying kindly:

"Joel, answer me; it seems to me that you are worse than when I left you."

Joel endeavored to raise himself, but in vain. His strength was so far exhausted that though he strove to speak he could not utter a word.

"He has grown worse rapidly, and ere sundown he will be gathered to his fathers," said the soldier who had been left to guard him.

Daniel sighed deeply, then placing his hand under the wounded man's head, raised it slightly,
saying :

" Speak, friend ! let me know your last wishes,
and I swear to fulfil them at the cost of my life."

At these words a joyful expression passed over
the face of the dying warrior, and making a violent
effort, he stammered :

" Sara . . . . Oh, to see her, and then to die ! ·'

"You shall see her," said Daniel, and without delay he started off to carry out the last earnest wish
of his friend.   •

Joel's house was at a long distance from the Fortress Antonia ; but Daniel, although wearied out by
the fatigue of the day, ran the whole way, through
his eager desire of satisfying Joel, so that he quickly
reached Sara's dwelling. But before knocking at
the door he halted upon the threshold to regain
breath and courage, for he was about to fulfil his sorrowful errand. He shuddered at the thought of the
despair of the poor wife, and was uncertain how to
announce to her the misfortune which had befallen
her. Then reflecting that every moment's delay
might prevent her from again seeing her dying
spouse, he mastered his emotion, and approaching
the door, knocked gently, but received no answer.

Fearing that some dire calamity might have cc-curred in the house where Anna dwelt, he knocked again more loudly, crying out:

"Anna! Sara! it is I! open to me! I come at Joel's request!" Scarcely had he pronounced that name when the door immediately opened and he beheld the daughter of Simon, who exclaimed joy-fully:

"Is that you, Daniel?"

"Yes, it is I, who am perhaps unwelcome," an-swered the young man bitterly, then added: "Where is Sara? I must speak with her."

"Follow me!" replied the maiden, furtively dry-ing a tear called forth by Daniel's harshness.

Daniel followed her, and halted in surprise on the threshold of the adjoining room, seeing the great disorder which reigned therein. The household goods lay on the ground, broken into a thousand pieces; the floor was stained with oil and strewn with wheat; Sara pressed Jonathan to her breast as if seeking to hide him in her bosom; and Maria, with bewildered looks, distorted features, dishevel-led hair, and arms extended above her head, held her infant in a threatening attitude.

"Here is a friend who has come from Joel," said Anna, to re-assure her companions.

"From Joel!" shrieked Sara, running towards Daniel; then continued: "Had my husband been here he would have protected us from the zealots, who came hither this morning and robbed us of the greater part of our wheat, oil, and other provisions; the wretches would have left us nothing had not Anna succeeded in concealing from them the few articles of food which remain to us."

"The zealots came here?" said Daniel, turning pale with dismay. Then he looked anxiously in Anna's face; but perceiving that the maiden's countenance, although pallid, was quite serene, he took courage, and pressing the hand of Joel's wife, endeavored to tell her why he had come; but his words failed him, and his voice was stifled in his throat.

"Why did not Joel accompany you?" asked Sara, anxiously.

"Joel is ill, and awaits you near the Fortress Antonia," replied Daniel.

"He is wounded, then? Speak, I implore you!" cried Sara.

"Follow me and you will see," answered Daniel.

The poor woman wrung her hands in despair, but her eyes were dry and her speech failed her, so great was the agony which filled her heart.

6*

Daniel would have preferred to see her weep and lament loudly; her silent sorrow terrified him. He nevertheless endeavored to console her; and supporting her tottering steps drew her towards the door, saying: "Take courage, Joel will recover; but we must hasten to him."

"I will accompany Sara," said Anna, taking Jonathan by the hand.

"The boy's tears will disturb Joel," resumed Daniel, making a sign to the maiden to remain behind.

"He is then dying?" asked Sara, in a hollow voice.

Daniel did not answer, but walked towards the door; and Sara, before following him, drew near Anna, saying:

"Swear to me in the name of our ancient friendship that, should I never return, you will be a mother to my son; swear it to me, I beseech you!"

"My religion prohibits me from swearing, for it is not in my power to make one hair black or white;* but I promise you by my father's memory that death alone shall separate me from Jonathan," answered the weeping girl; and then added: "Do not despair, dear friend; God will have pity on your husband, and will restore him to health."

* Matt. v. 36

Sara sadly shook her head and followed Daniel, who, finding that Anna would not look at him, withdrew more melancholy than he had come.

The two friends hurried rapidly along the street which led to the fortress, and had already accomplished more than half of the distance, when a Hebrew warrior came running towards Daniel, shouting to him :

"Our brethren are issuing from the walls to burn the enemy's engines; hear their shouts!"

Daniel made an angry gesture, thinking that the cry of war was ever calling him from beside his friends at the very moments in which he could be of service to them; but that call was too imperious to be resisted, for it was the cry of his country summoning her children to her defence. Pointing to Sara the place where Joel lay, he begged her to bow her head in submission to the will of Him who exalts and who humbles; then followed the soldier who had brought him the news of the Jewish proceedings.

Left alone, the wife of Joel hurried towards the spot indicated by Daniel, and found the wounded man alone, lying extended on the ground, exposed to the full force of the burning sun.

"Great God, he is dying!" exclaimed the wretched woman.

That voice, which would have re-animated Joel's dead bones even when lying in the depths of the tomb, quickened the pulsations of his dying heart. Opening his eyes he fixed them upon his beloved wife, smiling sweetly upon her, whilst she, leaning over her departing spouse, bathed his face with her tears, repeating distractedly:

" Do not die, Joel, do not die!"

A tear coursed down Joel's cheek; he had fancied, poor fellow! that Sara's presence would have sweetened his death agony; but at that moment he felt that the despair of his wife embittered the approach of that inexorable destroyer which was to tear him from his loved one in the very flower of his age. He made an effort to speak, and said in a feeble voice: "Sara, . . let . . . . me die with my head . . . . resting upon your . . . . knees."

Sara seated herself upon the ground, turning her back to the sun, in order to shield the dying man from its rays, and raising his head, laid it gently on her knees. A contented expression passed over Joel's face. Having obtained the desired position he seemed as if about to sink into a placid slumber; but shortly after he moved, a convulsive shudder passed over his limbs, and he stammered with great difficulty:

" I am thirsty . . . . my throat is so parched."

Sara looked around to see if there were some soldiers near, of whom she might ask the favor to fill
the earthen cup which lay empty beside Joel; but she
perceived no one and sat for some moments in indecision, not wishing to quit her dying husband; then
unable to witness his suffering, she ran towards
some soldiers who were grouped before the fortress,
and held her cup to them, crying out:

" A little water for a dying man! "

Those tiger-hearted men roughly answered her
that there was but very little of it, and that a dying
man had no further need of drinking.

" Water for Joel, who lies dying! " repeated the
poor woman, and the soldiers again repulsed her,
mocking her with bursts of noisy laughter.

The woes of Jerusalem had hardened all hearts.
Every day people died of hunger and thirst, so that
humanity, by force of cruel habit, was everywhere
extinguished; for if there be ever a time in which
evil passions, especially egotism, show themselves in
all their ugliness, it is when a great calamity weighs
upon a nation; then every one thinks only of his
own salvation, of his own wants, and pays little
heed to the necessities of his neighbors.

Finding scorn instead of pity, Sara's agony gave

way to fury, and extending her arms towards the
soldiers, she exclaimed :

"May you be accursed, since you refuse even a
drop of water to the dying! May the Divine
wrath overthrow the walls which you strive to defend, and may you be sold by the Romans as useless sheep."

Then turning her back upon the wretches who
derided her, she returned to Joel's side; he, tormented with thirst, begged for drink, not perceiving in his agony how much suffering he caused
Sara.

Prostrate on the ground the wretched woman tore
her hair, and would joyfully have given her life for
a cup of water. Suddenly an idea entered her
mind: she had seen a dagger lying on the ground,
and ran to pick it up; then raised the sleeve of her
dress and opened one of the veins of her arm with
the weapon; and as the blood slowly flowed into the
cup, a smile of cruel satisfaction broke upon her
lips. When she saw the cup almost filled, she
handed it to Joel.

The dying man swallowed a few drops of the tepid
liquid; oh! had he known that it was his wife's
heart's blood! The poor fellow, shortly after, bowed
his head upon his breast and calmly expired.

The bereaved widow called him by every loving name, but in vain, for the dead man's lips were mute: mute forever.

An utter prostration of strength succeeded to Sara's delirium; she soon ceased to suffer; her mental faculties failed her; and weakened by the loss of blood, which oozed slowly from her open wound, she fell dying beside her deceased spouse.

The hour of sunset is always melancholy, but on that day it was sadder than ever; for the last rays of the sun shone upon numerous corpses, which would never more behold its rising, and reflected full upon those of Sara and Joel, who, laid one beside the other, seemed as if asleep; their youthful faces wore so serene an aspect, now that they were freed from all earthly anxieties. When Daniel returned from the fight he would have thought his friends were sleeping, had not the blood in which they were bathed told him of some fatal catastrophe.

With eyes filled with tears Daniel looked at the two spouses who were reposing only to awaken upon the day of final judgment, when the trumpet of the angel of the resurrection should summon them to the Valley of Jehoshaphat, and said sobbingly:

"You died together, O you unfortunate ones! and the same tomb shall receive your remains."

So saying, he took an iron shovel which had been used to work at the defences, and went towards a little plot of ground situated beyond the Fortress Antonia, where lay numerous bodies piled one upon another; on seeing which Daniel thought that these unhappy beings, dying perhaps of hunger, had not had even a relative nor friend to bury them; then he began to dig a grave large enough to contain two bodies, and when completed he returned to bring his departed friends' remains thither.

He first attempted to raise Sara; but fancying that a sad expression passed over the countenance of Joel, he stopped, saying:

"Death carried you both off at once, and I will not separate you;" and bending down he also raised Joel's body in his arms.

The weight of the two corpses was not too much for the robust shoulders and broad breast of the valiant warrior, but it was difficult for him to walk encumbered by so inconvenient a burden; nevertheless he was proceeding onward, when behold, a man in appearance like an artisan, who was walking with slow and regular steps towards the tower, came near him, and stopping suddenly, as if some supernatural force constrained him to do so, said in a faint voice:

" Share your burden with me ; I must assist you."

Daniel did not refuse the offer, which was very acceptable to him, and thanking the stranger, laid Sara's body in his arms, and continued his journey, stopping only on the brink of the grave, in which he first placed Joel's corpse, then that of Sara. After casting a lingering look upon his unfortunate friends, he covered them with sand, exclaiming amid his sobs :

" Sleep in peace, loving hearts! and may your native earth lie lightly upon your tomb!"

After drying the tears which fell from his eyes, he turned to thank the stranger ; but he no longer saw him ; he was already far in the distance, saying, as if speaking to himself: " Blessed are those whose journey through this life is ended, and who repose in the tomb."

CHAPTER XII.

THE condition of Jerusalem became still more terrible; so that all might envy the fate of Sara and Joel, who were prevented by death from witnessing the fearful calamities of their country.

The Romans, discouraged by the desperate fury of the Jews, who were successful in burning their engines of war, soon perceived that they would have to struggle to the last with a people rendered strong by despair, ere they could dream of taking Jerusalem. Nevertheless, Titus did not lose hope. He was certain of victory; and wishing to hasten it in order to spare unnecessary carnage, he re-united his legions within the enclosures of the walls already in his possession, and surrounded the city with a barricade which extended from the Mount of Olives to the brook Cedron, and cut off from the inhabit ants every means of procuring food, depriving them even of the roots and herbs which the unfortu nate wretches, urged on by hunger, were used to dig in the adjacent valleys.

The disastrous fate of the city condemned by God grew worse, beyond the power of the most able pen to describe. The accounts given of it would seem exaggerated or fabulous, had not the Jewish historian, who was an eye-witness of the facts, left us a full history of it.

Since the beginning of the siege, hunger had crept in among the besieged; but since Titus had so closely barricaded the city, it had reached its climax. The granaries which had furnished food to the citizens had been sacked and burned by the swords men; the herds of cattle daily decreased, and all kinds of provisions were exhausted, so that were any bushels of wheat yet to be found, they were sold at an enormous price, and even pounded hay served as food, and was purchased at the price of wheat.

The zealots stormed those houses which they supposed to contain food, and, like famished tigers, took possession of whatever they could find, murdering and maltreating the owners in the most barbarous and inhuman manner.

Every tie of relationship and friendship was disregarded; every sentiment of piety was extinguished; the brother, rendered frantic by the delirium caused by hunger and abusing his manly strength, wrested

from his sister's hand her last crumb of bread,
which only served to prolong his painful existence
for a few hours; the husband snatched the food
from his dying wife, had she, more fortunate than
himself, been able to procure it; the friend murdered
his friend to obtain a root or a morsel of pounded
hay; so that death, less ferocious than hunger, was
the fate reserved for those who had with difficulty
procured a little nourishment for themselves.

Everything seemed to allay the hunger of that
people overwhelmed by the curse of heaven. Hay
was a banquet fit for Lucullus; the sweepings of the
streets were carefully examined in hopes of finding
some few straws or dried leaves; the skins of animals and the sinews of beasts already long dead
were eagerly devoured. Happy was he who could find
the sole of an old shoe! he hid himself to conceal
his treasure. The filthiest things were eagerly sought
after; and what would formerly have seemed repul-
sive, then became not only grateful to the palate,
but its possessor was obliged even to sustain a fierce
struggle to succeed in devouring it, for all disputed
it with him.

The brigands ransacked every corner; and could
they find a piece of meat yet raw or just placed before the fire, they would instantly snatch it; and

not content with that, they descended into the sewers to see if provisions were hidden therein ; opened the tombs, profaning the bones of the dead ! . . . . in short, hungry rage drove them to all manner of unheard-of and guilty excesses.

Many families perished of hunger ; men, women, children, and old men dragging themselves with difficulty along the streets in search of food, and with livid faces, bewildered looks, and stomachs distended by suffering and by the miasma exhaling from the corpses, walked along in sullen silence, not having strength to complain ; and when they fell, were unable to rise, and dying, added to the number of those already poisoning the air.

Jerusalem had become the city of the dead. The houses, the terraces, the cellars, and the streets were encumbered with unburied corpses, besides those which were occasionally thrown beyond the walls by the zealots, so that the counter-drains were filled with dead, whose stench was fatal even to the Romans. The victims of hunger amounted already to two hundred thousand, besides those carried off by pestilence.

But more cruel than either famine or plague was that handful of rebels, who, whilst their brethren were fighting, wandered throughout the city, aban-

douing themselves to the most unbridled licentious-
ness, and murdering those poor wretches from whom
they could take nothing, because they had nothing
to lose.

Many Jerusalemites, driven to desperation, threw
themselves from the walls, and numbers perished in
so doing; but those who could save themselves by
falling upon the corpses piled up beneath, sought
the Roman camp only to find death in a more cruel
form; for devouring with frantic avidity the food
with which the pitying enemy supplied them, they
were scarcely satiated with bread and meat ere
they would fall to the ground a prey to severe pains,
which gnawed their vitals—for their stomachs, weakened by long fasting, had not the strength to digest;
and the poor creatures died amid horrible convul-
sions, accusing the Romans of having poisoned them.

The combatants seeing from the walls the painful
deaths of their brethren, rejoiced greatly, consider-
ing it a punishment of Heaven for having aban
doned the city at so calamitous a moment, and
seeking refuge in the abhorred Roman camp.

During the day the streets of Jerusalem presented
an aspect of the utmost desolation, and at night they
were as silent as the grave, for the brigands assem-
bled upon the walls, and the inhabitants of the be-

sieged city found in sleep, or rather in a lethargic
stupor, the momentary forgetfulness of their sufferings.

Five days after the deaths of Sara and of Joel, as
the moon was shining upon the putrid streets of
Jerusalem, which were strewn with fetid corpses,
the man who by the shores of Lake Asphaltites had
buried Simon, and who had appeared to Daniel
under the guise of an artisan, was advancing
towards Herod's palace. Walking with his usual
slow and regular step, and without stopping, he
turned his head now to one side, now to the other,
to look at the dead bodies which lined the road.

An expression of ruthless melancholy overspread
the countenance of the mysterious man, who was no
thinner than when we first saw him ; as if hunger,
merciless to all others, had passed lightly over him ;
and the miasma of the plague-laden air, and the
fierce sufferings of the besieged, had in no way
affected his health nor diminished his strength.

Alone, wandering like a spectre amid the dead,
whom he watched with an envious eye, he sighed
deeply whenever his glance fell upon the edifices
which had either been burned or destroyed by the
zealots, as if he wept far more over the destruction
of the monuments of the city of David than over

the sad fate of her children. However, did he meet one of the inhabitants issuing secretly from his house, and searching among the dead bodies in hopes of finding some nourishment, then the nocturnal traveller would close his eyes to avoid witnessing the sufferings of a living being.

The night was already far spent, and he had never once stopped, when he passed before the corpse of a man lying on the ground, his rigid hand clasped tightly around his throat, as if he had strangled himself to shorten his painful agony. Then the artisan trembled from head to foot, and continuing his unceasing walk, said sorrowfully, as he turned his head behind to look at the deceased:

"Son of my son, I cannot stop to lay you in the tomb; had I seen you in the arms of a man, I could have taken you into my own, and, thereby relieving a living man of his burden, could have buried you."

Then crossing his arms he bowed his head on his breast and passed onwards. But after a few more steps, he shuddered anew at the sight of a woman, who, lately dead, lay stretched on the ground, with open mouth, and face stained by black spots, and even in death strained to her breast a little babe, who, still alive, was vainly seeking nourishment from the maternal bosom.

Without pausing, the artisan raised the sucking child, and wrapping it in his doublet, endeavored to warm its tender limbs; but in vain, for the little creature threw up its arms and expired without a moan.

A tear coursed down the stranger's cheek; and reaching the atrium of a house where stood a marble basin, he laid the infant therein, and departed, saying:

" Rest in peace, last scion of a guilty race! I saw your father and your mother die of hunger; you, happier than they, did not bear the weight of my sin, and expired ere you could understand the trials of this valley of tears. Sleep in peace, and may that Just One, whom I dare not name, have pity on you who couldst not have known Him."

So saying, he went on his way; he walked aimlessly, taking a thousand turnings, and his steps were ever slow and regular; it seemed as if his feet were driven onward against his will. When he reached the house of Pilate a sob burst from his lips, then, apparently unwillingly, he took the road which led from the Roman Pro-Consulate to Golgotha. After going a short distance, his face suddenly became convulsed, his limbs trembled nervously, and his eyes fell as if by some fascination upon a

7

half-razed house of mean appearance, whose win
dows, doors, and walls were falling to ruin.   A wild
fig-tree, destitute of leaves, for the stalk had been
stripped by the famished Jews, has taken root in the
cracks of the walls below the battlements, and its
branches concealed the nest of an owl, which, as tho
traveller paused before it, took to flight, flapping its
wings.

The whole place wore a baleful look ; it seemed
as if the curse of heaven hung on it, it was so
squalid and desolate.

On reaching the threshold of the wretched habi
tation, the artisan covered his face with his hands to
shut it from his sight, and exclaimed amid his sobs:

"There is the house wherein I first saw the
light ! . . . There is the spot where I was so culpable ! "   Then extending his arms towards heaven:
"Almighty Avenger," he said, "great is thy justice, terrible thy wrath . . . Thou urged my feet
towards Jerusalem, in order that I may witness the
destruction of my country, and the slaughter of my
brethren.   My steps, led on by thy will, carried me
whither my son's son and his wife lay dead from
hunger ; and I held the remains of the last of my
descendants within my arms, unable to dig for him
a last resting-place . . . Eternal God, tremendous

is thy anger, but thy mercy is infinite, since it chas-
tizes me in this world to save me throughout eternity ! ... Days pass away, years roll around, centuries end, my punishment will be long ; but everything finishes here below, and at last I may find
rest after having expiated my sin ... Be thou there
fore blessed, in thy infinite mercy, and do not close
thy ears against a sinner who from the depths of his
misery cries to thee, invoking thy pity ... !"

The sad monologue ended, he remained silent,
for he was now far from the spot so rich to him in
painful memories. He continued walking the
whole night, without stopping for one moment,
through the heaps of corpses which seemed yet
more horrible in the pale moonlight.

At sunrise he was still wandering ; the wheel
of time was to make innumerable turns ere he
should be given the repose for which he so earnestly
longed.

CHAPTER XIII.

ANNA had vainly awaited the return of her two friends; five days passed, a week rolled on, and no tidings either of Sara or Joel, who were never more to be seen in this world.

The poor child was greatly distressed at their absence, not knowing the cause, and several times resolved to repair to the ·Fortress Antonia to seek some news regarding them, but the fear of exposing herself to the insults of the swordsmen had deterred her. Besides which, she could not bear to separate herself from Jonathan even for one single moment.

The hours thus passed in constant anxiety seemed terribly long to her. Every evening, as she retired, she would say to herself, "I shall see them to-morrow!" But the morrow destroyed her hopes and augmented her distress; for the fear that Daniel also might be dead, added greatly ·to her anguish. Nevertheless she contrived to overcome her sorrow and regain her courage. Being gifted with one of those characters which, timid in the ordinary cir

ɔumstances of life, become energetic and fearless
in moments of difficulty.

Forgetful of her own sufferings she became daily
more attached to Jonathan, for whom she wished to
live in order to fulfil the promise made to her bene-
factress, namely, to become a mother to the little
orphan, who, like herself, still longed for the return
of Sara and Joel.

Added to the agony caused by Sara's absence,
was the fear of hunger, which began to make itself
felt. The wheat and oil which the maiden had concealed from the rapacious zealots, were consumed,
although they were used with the most rigid
economy.

Three days since, the last remnants of the provisions had been exhausted. On the first day, Anna
went out in search of food, and, after some delay,
had found an old woman, who, tempted by an exor-
bitant recompense, had sold her a cake of meal
cooked for more than a month, and so hard that it
could only be eaten after being long soaked in
water.

Fortunately Anna had money, and buying the
cake, she joyfully hastened home, and shared it
among the three famished beings who were awaiting her, weeping with impatience; for Maria,

although she had partly recovered her reason, was thrown into a state of delirious frenzy whenever she felt the craving pangs of hunger.

All that day she thought not of her friend's absence, for the affectionate girl dearly loved the orphan boy, and for his sake shuddered at the idea of death, which, were it not for him, she would have gladly welcomed; then, too, not only did the son of her beloved Sara occupy her mind, but likewise poor Maria and her nursing babe; so that we may readily imagine the burden these three persons were to her, in that cruel situation where one person could barely find food for herself, and that with great difficulty.

The hard cake had only been sufficient for one day; and on the succeeding morning, Anna had no more money, and knew not whither to turn to procure a little food.

Wearied with long watching, during which she had racked her brain to discover some means of saving her friends from starvation, the maiden prepared to leave the house in search of nourishment; but first cast her eyes towards heaven, begging her father to pray to the Almighty for her who, alone and defenceless, was exposed to falling into the hands of the swordsmen; and likewise besought Him who

tempers the wind to the shorn lamb, that He would
give her strength and courage to live without murmuring at her misfortunes.

Upon quitting her dwelling, her first thought
was to go in search of Daniel; but reflecting that
perhaps at that very moment her early friend lay an
unburied corpse, she turned her steps elsewhere, and
walking slowly along, looked carefully between the
stones of the walls of the buildings to see if there was
possibly some fibres of roots; but all in vain, for every
place had already been explored outside as well as
inside, and not even the smallest atom of straw could
be found.

Occasionally Anna stopped to avoid treading
upon a corpse, and changing her path, turned towards some other part of the city, or followed a
crowd of men who, silent and staggering, wandered
into solitary places in search of wild roots; but seeing that they found nothing, she abandoned them to
follow others still more unfortunate.

For some time the poor girl's endeavors were
vain, and discouragement gradually took possession
of her mind; for as it grew late she thought of
Jonathan and Maria who were awaiting her return.
Not knowing of whom to ask aid, since almost all
the Jerusalemites were equally destitute with herself,

she suddenly found herself near the pool of Siloam but previous to reaching it her attention was drawn to a man who lay dead on the ground, straining to his breast a parcel wrapped in a woollen cloth.

Although the corpse inspired her with extreme repugnance, Anna overcame herself and took from the dead man's hand the bundle which he had perhaps clenched in his agony, and a scream of joy issued from her lips at the sight of a large loaf which fell from the wrappings; but at the same instant, a half-naked man, with a cadaverous and meagre countenance, coming out of a half-ruined house, rushed towards her, and striving to snatch the bread which she had picked up from the ground, cried out:

"I saw you!"

It would not have been difficult for Anna to push away that man—who stood tottering as if quite unable to keep on his feet—and was about doing so, when he, finding himself unable to overcome the resistance which she made, exclaimed in tones of the utmost despair:

"My mother is dying of hunger! I have vainly striven to nourish her with my own blood; she is dying!"

Anna's arms fell nervelessly, and her hands drop-

ped the bread which they had so lately clutched.
The son's cry had deprived her of energy, pity par-
alyzed her strength ; and covering her eyes to avoid
seeing the poor wretch who fled away with his
prize, she remained motionless. But almost imme
diately a cruel re-action succeeded to her sudden
burst of pity ; tearing her hair, she blamed herself
for the weakness which had led her to have compassion upon a stranger, whilst the son of her benefac-
tress was dying of hunger.

She stood for some moments weeping despairingly ; finally drying her tears she turned towards Sara's
house ; but after a few steps, she saw a bundle of
roots lying on the ground, and hastily picked them
up, thanking Divine Providence for having aided her
Then hiding her treasure, lest it might be wrested
from her, she hurried to her house, and pressing the
little orphan to her bosom, said to him joyfully :

" To-day, at least, you shall not die of hunger ! "

" What have you brought us, then ? " said Maria,
seizing the arm of the maiden, who answered :

" I found a bundle of roots, which I will cook
with oil."

Maria made an angry gesture, tore her clothes,
and muttered between her teeth, as she crouched in
a corner of the room :

"The ox and the goat eat grass and roots, but I and my son need bread to satisfy our hunger."

Anna shuddered, fearing that the insane creature, tormented by hunger, might commit some crime; and hastily cooked the roots as best she might, then gave some to Maria, who would not taste it; and perceiving that her babe also refused the food, she burst into loud screams and lamentations.

Until evening the poor woman wept incessantly; and with gestures, by turns threatening and beseeching, begged for bread, thereby agonizing Anna, who with great difficulty succeeded in calming her and persuading her to lie down, promising her that she should have all that she required on the morrow.

Whilst Maria slept, Anna sat at the foot of Jonathan's little couch, thinking that on the following day she must wander anew in search of something to satisfy the hunger of the three wretched beings who had no one save her to look to upon earth, and that perhaps all her researches would be vain. Although such thoughts were painful, still she did not lose courage, and even thanked God for having led her to Jerusalem to become the protector of Sara' orphan boy.

Anna continued her vigils until morning, and at sunrise she was about starting on her pilgrimage, but first awoke Maria to tell her to keep quiet until her return. Maria sprang to her feet, and taking the young girl's hand, asked in a harsh voice:

"Where is the bread?"

"I have none, dear sister; but I will try by all means in my power to procure some," replied Anna, sighing sadly.

"Bread, bread!" screamed the crazy woman.

"Be quiet, Maria, and if you are good and reasonable, when I return I will bring you some," said the maiden, gently.

Maria angrily stamped on the ground, and began weeping, and after raving for some time, seated herself, saying:

"Very well, I will wait patiently, but be quick, and woe be to you if you return empty-handed."

Anna knew not what to answer, and turned towards the door; but Jonathan ran to her, and pulling her gown, said to her:

"Anna, take me with you, and do not leave me alone with Maria; she frightens me terribly when you are not here."

Anna, not wishing to expose the child unnecessarily to danger, endeavored to persuade him to remain; but Jonathan sobbed violently, and refused to be separated from his adopted mother.

Suddenly Maria rose from her seat, and appi oach-ing the boy, cried out in threatening tones: " Be quiet, if you do not wish me to strangle you with my hands ! Your complaints will awaken my son."

Anna then raised Jonathan in her arms, and as she carried him away with her, fearing to leave him in Maria's power, she kissed him several times, saying lovingly :

" Henceforth you shall never leave my side; and if we must die, we will die together."

All that day poor Anna wandered about, finding nothing; and towards evening, although sick and weary, she had not courage to return to her house, fearing Maria's desperation. At last, unable to remain longer on her feet, she turned her steps homeward, and on reaching their dwelling, stood bewildered at the sight of a number of people who were gathering before it. Not knowing what to think, she made her way through the crowd, which was composed of brigands and women, who with dishevelled hair, ragged clothing, and meagre looks, seemed like so many spectres who had wandered from the infernal regions.

All those people were screaming and pointing to-wards the house, and amid their cries the maiden could distinguish these words constantly repeated .

"Let us force open the door! Let us kill those who eat whilst we are dying of hunger! Smell, smell the odor of cooked flesh!"

Anna trembled with fear, and endeavored to speak to the people, to tell them that there was no one in the house save a poor crazy woman; but no one listened to her, and the crowd urging her onwards, pressed her closely against the barred entrance.

"Let us tear down the door!" cried the brigands; and were about carrying their threat into execution when the door suddenly opened and Maria appeared in full sight. She looked like one of the Furies. For a moment the crowd kept silence, in order to hear the words which she, with a laugh which chilled all with horror, and extending her arms towards the multitude, said in a harsh voice:

"Come in, and take your share of the sumptuous banquet which I have prepared for you."

The crowd rushed into the house in search of that meat the nauseous smell of which had attracted them; but very quickly a scream of horror broke from the lips of all at the sight of Maria, who, standing upon the threshold of the adjoining room, held high above her head the roasted body of a little boy, already half eaten.

The cry of horror was succeeded by profound si

lence, and every one looked at the crazy woman, who, waving the corpse, screamed in her delirium :

" Eat, eat ! Do not be more compassionate than a mother who, urged on by hunger, devoured her child to avoid hearing his cries. Eat, eat ! You murdered my husband, you robbed me of my wealth; now satiate yourselves on the remains of my son ! " *

The crowd did not reply ; the horrible action had terrified the' minds of all ; but suddenly a voice broke the deep and fatal silence, saying :

" May she be accursed ! and may the malediction of Heaven raze the house from top to bottom ! "

At these words the multitude rushed forth from Anna's dwelling, as if fearing to see it immediately crumble.

" Death to the cruel wretch ! " cried all ; and Anna, utterly unable to save the poor demented creature, strained Jonathan to her bosom in an agony of tears.

Suddenly two swordsmen, each bearing a lighted torch, re-entered the house, and shortly after came

---

* Flavius Josephus. in his " History of the Jewish Wars," thus relates the above mentioned fact " She killed her son. and roasting the body, devoured one-half. hiding the remainder; but the swordsmen. attracted by the smell of the accursed food. threatened to murder her if she did not give them that which she had prepared; and she. telling them that she had a sumptuous banquet for them, showed them the remains of her child," etc., etc.

oat, closing the door of entrance; and the crowd, forgetting the hunger which tormented them, furiously applauded, crying:

" Let the wretch die roasted like her infant ! "

The flames quickly opened for themselves an egress through the door and between the window-frames. Anna, pale and with terrified looks, fled from the fatal and accursed spot, exclaiming:

" Almighty God ! judge not that poor unhappy creature in thy anger, nor correct her in thy wrath ! "

The crowd did not quit the house until it was entirely consumed, and nothing remained of the poor crazy woman save a handful of ashes.

Meanwhile Anna fled onwards, a prey to intense sorrow, now that she had no dwelling-place, without food, weakened by fasting and fatigue. She had not even a place wherein to lay down her head and die in peace.

For some time the wretched girl wandered about without knowing where she was going; but seeing that Jonathan, who had no .onger strength to walk, clung weeping to her knees, she took him in her arms and seated herself on the ground in a spot which the thick darkness prevented her from recog nizing.

Jonathan, overcome by fatigue, slept in the arms of his adopted mother; but the latter, although quite worn out, could not close her eyes. Her mind being weakened by so many and such varied emotions, she became delirious, and in her delirium saw Maria, who angrily showed her the corpse of her murdered child. This frightful vision passing away, another succeeded to it, in which Daniel, appearing to her clothed in rich apparel, invited her to seat herself at a sumptuous nuptial banquet.

The delirium lasted for some time. At last nature could bear no more, and she fell senseless to the ground, still clasping Jonathan in her arms. Without knowing it, she lay extended upon the tomb of Sara and of Joel.

CHAPTER XIV.

THROUGHOUT the entire night Anna remained unconscious, and only recovered from her lethargy about daybreak, but she was utterly unable to rise from the ground where she lay. She knew where she was, and heard the cries of Jonathan, who kept continually calling her, but was too weak to answer him. For three days she had eaten nothing, having given her share of the roots to her little charge. Her state would have rapidly grown worse had not Providence, under the form of a soldier, come to her assistance.

A man clad and armed after the fashion of the Hebrew soldiers, and who, although in Jewish costume, bore a very short beard, paused before the maiden, his head bent, as if deep in meditation. Occupied with his own thoughts, he would not have noticed the reclining figure, had not the cries of the child attracted his attention. Then approaching Jonathan, he caressed him, saying compassionately:

"Do not weep, poor innocent; your mother can no longer hear you."

"She hears me, but she will not answer me," replied the child between his sobs.

The soldier laid his hand on Anna's heart to feel its pulsations, then brushed away the hair which hung dishevelled over the pallid features, and said wonderingly:

"If I am not mistaken, this is the woman who accompanied me under the walls of Jerusalem and who disappeared whilst my fellow-citizens assailed me with their javelins. Poor girl! probably she is starving to death."

Uttering these words, the soldier kneeled beside her, and taking from a pouch hanging from the girdle of his doublet a small gourd filled with honeyed wine and a large fresh meal cake, forced Anna to swallow a good portion of the wine, and breaking the cake into bits gave her some of it to eat; doing the same for Jonathan, who with greedy eyes watched his adopted mother, who, gradually recovering herself, could already eat without the assistance of the kind soldier.

After Anna had taken some more wine, her strength somewhat returned; and rising she turned to thank him who had so opportunely come to her

assistance, and looking him full in the face, immediately recognized him, notwithstanding the loss of his
beard, and exclaimed:

"You here, Flavius?"

Flavius Josephus knitted his eye-brows, and
glanced angrily at the questioner as if displeased at
being known; then soon recovering his temper, he
smiled, saying:

"You have a perspicacious eye, maiden; but if
you would not be the means of my death, nor are
anxious that your fellow-citizens should add to their
many crimes that of the murder of their former
general, tell no one that you have seen me. I came
hither in this disguise, not to speak with John of
Giscala—for he hates me, and my voice would sound
unpleasantly in his ears—but to give advice to many
who are fighting under his orders. Now all resistance is foolish and wicked; the city of Jerusalem is
strewn with corpses; the dead far outnumber the
living, and all prolonged opposition will render the
Sion a mass of corruption and a heap of ruins. But
time is precious," he added, sighing deeply, as he
thought over the misfortunes of his country, "I must
leave you. Should I succeed in escaping safely from
the walls which still protect the Temple, you shall
accompany me to the Roman camp; but should you

not see me again, you may conclude that I am dead, and that my remains augment the number of the hecatombs which divine wrath requires from our nation in expiation of our sins."

Josephus departed. Anna remained deep in thought, while Jonathan, seated upon the ground, amused himself with the stones which lay upon the grave of his parents. The maiden was sad, for, although partly glad to leave Jerusalem in order to preserve the precious life of her orphan charge, she felt unhappy at the idea of quitting her native land without hearing something of Daniel, without knowing if he were still among the combatants or already numbered with the dead; she then fully realized that misfortune and danger had greatly augmented the affection which she felt for the friend of her childhood; and weeping bitterly, besought her father to pardon her that sentiment which, innocent and chaste, was stronger than her good resolutions to overcome it.

She wept for some time without however murmuring against the divine will which condemned her to tears at so early an age; then folding her arms on her breast and watching Jonathan, who continued to play in the sand, she awaited the return of Flavius Josephus. But in vain; for John of Giscala suspecting that an emissary of the Romans was wandering among his soldiers to induce them to surrender, made so strict a search for him that Flavius could with great difficulty save himself by flight, without being able to fulfil the promise made to the daughter of Simon.

Not seeing him arrive, Anna supposed him to be dead, and sincerely regretted his fate; then, unable to remain longer in such a state of uncertainty, she climbed to the top of a little hill from the summit of which she could see the Fortress Antonia, the Temple, and a considerable portion of the road which led to the valley where Sara and Joel were buried.

While the young girl stood looking anxiously in the direction from which Flavius was to approach, she suddenly started in terror on hearing the noise of the battering-ram, which hurled its iron missiles against the walls of the fortress.

The warlike machine continued its work for several hours, and a large portion of the walls crumbled to the ground; but the Romans were greatly surprised when they saw that a wall far more solid than the former one rose behind the breach. The Jews had not been idle during the siege, but had erected this other almost impregnable bulwark. The enemy were greatly discouraged, and murmured loudly, say ing that the Jews, like the hundred-headed Hydra, were indestructible; but, re-animated by the voice of Titus, twelve soldiers rushed forward, and, without waiting orders, began to scale the walls, resolved either to die or to conquer.[*]

From afar Anna heard their shouts and watched their ascent, and likewise saw the Jews, who, terrified at the daring of their enemy, abandoned the defence in a dastardly manner. Such cowardice made her tremble with anger, and she was about shutting her eyes to avoid the sight of the defeat of her compatriots, when she perceived a warrior, who, encouraging his fellow-soldiers by his example, urged himself forward, and struggling with irresistible courage, threw down the foremost assailants, who were already about to set foot upon the conquered bulwark.

Anna watched with throbbing heart the valiant Israelite whose efforts hindered the Fortress Antonia from falling into the hands of the Romans. Trembling for his safety, she looked attentively at him, admiring his agile movements, which caused his brilliant armor to sparkle in the sun's rays; and a scream of joy echoed throughout the valley when in the valorous Jew she recognized her lamented

[*] Flavius Josephus' " Jewish Wars."

Daniel; then, stretching her arms towards him, she exclaimed:

"Courage, courage, my valiant brother! The enemy are few in number, and you can easily overcome them!"

Could Daniel have heard the cry of his beloved and beheld her pale face, he would no longer have doubted of the love which she bore him.

With her mind agitated by so many and such violent emotions, the maiden awaited the issue of the struggle; and when she perceived that victory had been favorable to the young warrior, she fervently thanked God; then continued to watch the victor, who, with his arms crossed on his breast, looked absently at the remains of the fallen Romans, and imprudently exposed himself to the javelins of the enemy, who sought to avenge the defeat of the soldiers.

Daniel exposed himself to death both carelessly and imprudently, for, having gone the previous evening to Sara's dwelling, and finding it entirely destroyed by fire, had concluded that Anna had perished in the flames. Driven to desperation, he had rushed to the tower-walls; but indignant at the pusillanimity of his companions-in-arms, he had sought ere dying to encourage them to repulse the

Romans. Until evening the maiden remained gaz
ing towards the tower, and when darkness prevented
her from seeing its walls, she seated herself upon
the ground, holding the sleeping Jonathan on her
knees, and feeling more tranquil because she seemed
no longer alone upon earth, since not far from her,
within range of her eyes, was Daniel, to whom she
could have recourse in case of extreme necessity.

Comforted by such pleasant thoughts, the young
maiden lay down upon the ground and slept quietly. God in his mercy sent her a delightful vision. She seemed to be walking through the streets
of a magnificent city wholly unknown to her, and
holding Jonathan by the hand—to be looking tearfully upon a triumphal arch which commemorated
the fall of her country and the slavery of her people; then, still dreaming, she seemed to descend
into an obscure subterranean, where amid the darkness she saw Daniel prostrate before the sign of the
Redemption, which alone shone brilliantly in the
gloomy cavern.

The poor girl slept until morning, favored by
happy dreams. Then awaking, her first thought
was to look towards the tower; and not seeing Daniel on its turrets, smiled to think that he was safe
from the enemy's darts.

Throughout that day and the one following she remained upon the hill, supporting herself as well as Jonathan with the provisions left her by Flavius Josephus, safe from the snares of the zealots, who did not venture to that deserted spot, and not saddened by the sight of the famishing creatures who filled the other streets. But on the third night, as she was quietly sleeping, she was awakened by a shout, sharp as the hissing of the wind passing between two mountains. Bewildered and uncertain what to do, she sprang to her feet, and soon heard fresh cries coming from the Fortress Antonia. They were the shouts of the victors mingled with the despairing groans of the vanquished.

In her bewilderment Anna supposed that the Romans had again attempted to scale the walls, but that repulsed by the Israelites they had fled away in confusion, uttering loud shouts; but she was strangely deceived, for the despairing groans came from the Jews, who, attacked by the enemy in the silence of night, overwhelmed with fright, abandoned all defence, flying precipitately without any thought of the few valiant warriors who, striving to offer some resistance, fell overpowered by the number of the assailants, fighting without order in a confused melee.

Anna trembled when she heard the imprecations

of the vanquished as they ran along the street leading to the Temple; and at the thought that Daniel
might fall a victim, she felt her strength fail her;
but the complaints of Jonathan, who clung weeping
to her knees, aroused all her energy; and reflecting
that the Romans might scatter themselves even as
far as the hill whereon she had found refuge, she
decided to repair to the Temple ere the vanquished
arrived there.

Breathless, dragging after her her little charge,
who could hardly walk from fatigue, she reached
the enclosure of the Temple, where were gathered
together an immense multitude of women and children, whilst the men prepared to defend it; for the
shouts of the conquerors had reached even the in-
nermost parts of the city, and the news of the
enemy's victory had become known to all.

At the moment in which Anna mingled with the
unarmed populace, who were groaning and rending
their clothes in sign of mourning, the Romans, em-
boldened by their former victory, followed the fugitives, and were about overtaking them, when the
latter, excited by the fear of losing the small portion of the city which yet remained to them, and
animated by the words of John of Giscala, turned
about, and endeavored to repulse the enemy.

The contest was a furious one; the Jews fought with indescribable courage; but their fate had already been apportioned by God. For a moment victory seemed favorable to them, but quickly turned against them.

Nevertheless the fight lasted several hours, and with such desperate resolution that the Romans. overpowered by numbers, were forced to recede and return to the conquered fortress, whilst the Israelites barricaded themselves in the fortified enclosure of the Temple, the last stronghold of the deicide nation.

CHAPTER XV.

MARVELOUS in its stupendous magnificence rose the Temple of Jerusalem; and the pilgrim repairing to that city, seeing from afar its gilded roof,* deemed it no human creation. But notwithstanding its beauty it was doomed to destruction, and the hand of a Roman soldier was to become the instrument of divine anger, and to kindle the first spark destined to reduce to ashes the most splendid edifice in the world. The Temple was to fall in ruins; and Jerusalem, according to the prediction of Jeremiah, was to become a heap of sand, a den of dragons, a desert!

The soldiers filled the porticos of the Temple, whose colossal columns of white marble upheld the ceiling of cedar-wood inlaid with gold and silver.

Women, old men, and children wandered weeping through the galleries; for almost all those who had survived the famine, the pestilence, and the general

---

* The roof was covered here and there with sharp golden spikes, to prevent the birds from lighting upon and soiling it.

slaughter, had sought refuge either in the Temple or in the southern part of the city.

The priests were gathered in the Holy of Holies—that is, in the two rooms overlaid within and without with gilded planks and having golden doors, in which were kept the seven branched candlesticks, with the other precious vessels—and there rending their vestments and covering their heads with ashes, they mourned over the misfortunes of the chosen people.

The Fortress Antonia being taken, Titus gave some days' truce to the besieged, to gain time to raze the tower to the ground, although from its wealth of marble and its majestic architecture it was one of the most beautiful edifices of Jerusalem ; then he introduced all his army into the last circuit of wall, through the breach made by its destruction, and prepared to attack the Temple, setting fire to the southern gate of the enclosure of the Sanctuary, to gain possession of the Court of Israel.

Although every way of escape was closed against the besieged, still they would not surrender, and like raging lions retired into the last Court of the Priests, which was defended by several towers and surrounded by a solid line of wall.   Here they resolved to hold out to the last, preferring in their heroic obstinacy to see the Sanctuary destroyed rather than to yield to the enemy.

Nothing now remained for the enemy to conquer save the interior of the Temple and the upper part of the city; therefore, secure of victory, they prepared to complete it, happy to end that exterminating war which had lasted for so long a time. But in vain did their military engines during many days thunder their projectiles against the walls of the court of the priests. Those impregnable fortifications remained unhurt, and the battering-rams were powerless against them.

Titus seeing that every attempt was fruitless, and that victory, hitherto favorable to his arms, stood halting before this last obstacle, ordered a scaling party to the attack. Then the Roman soldiers, animated by the voice of their beloved leader, placed their ladders against the walls, and, filled with martial enthusiasm, began to mount them; but they paid for their daring with death, for the besieged hurried to the spots where the ladders were planted, already crowded with the assailants, and overthrowing them, committed great havoc among the enemy.

Titus, lamenting the slaughter of so many valiant warriors, gave orders that they should set fire to those doors which opened into the porticos. They

were of cedar-wood and silver; but the metal liqui-
fying, the fire communicated itself to the wooden
ceiling, and for two days raged with undiminished
fury.

On the following days the fire still continued,
and increased every instant, until finally Titus, unable to witness the destruction of so much magnificence, caused it to be extinguished, and at the head
of his warriors entered the Court of the Priests,
proceeded as far as the altar of holocaust, which rose
opposite the gate of the Sanctuary, and there called
a council of the chiefs of his army.

Many voted for the total destruction of the Temple, urging that the Jews would never yield until
that building was razed to the ground; but Titus
opposed so barbarous a measure, and his opinion
prevailed over the others.

The day following the council convoked by Titus,
the Jews suddenly issued from the eastern or beautiful gate of the Temple, and with desperate energy
attacked the Romans, who after five hours' fighting
drove them back behind their defences. It was after
this battle that a Roman soldier, more daring than
the rest, leaping on the shoulders of his companion,
reached the level of one of the windows of the ninety-
nine halls which surrounded the Sanctuary, and flung

a lighted torch into the interior. The fire seized upon the hangings of fine linen, purple, and jacinth, which adorned it, and very shortly reached the ceiling.

Vainly did Titus give orders to extinguish the fire; no one listened to them. The soldiers, drunk with blood, wandered amid the flames in search of further victims. Then, at the risk of his own life, the Roman general entered the Holy of Holies, whither the fire had not yet penetrated, and saw with mixed surprise and admiration the seven-branched golden candlestick and the table of the showbread. Desirous to save so many and such precious articles, he again commanded the fire to be extinguished; but he spoke to the winds; the destiny of Jerusalem was to be accomplished!

From that fatal moment the victors did naught else but abandon themselves to plunder, to destruction, and to slaughter. The sacred vessels were broken, the priestly robes stolen. Nothing was respected by those exasperated wretches, who, greedy of booty, burned their own hands in tearing from the walls the plates of gold which had not already melted. Women, aged men, and children were murdered, and even those who threw down their arms and begged for mercy shared the same fate.

The crackling flames rose towards heaven, and the moans of the dying and the despairing screams of the women mingled with the shouts of frenzied joy uttered by the conquerors during their bloody orgie. The ground was covered by corpses; but the Romans, not satisfied with that, continued the carnage and pursued the fugitives who sought to save themselves in the lower part of the city.

Amid such havoc, Anna, carrying Jonathan on her shoulders, sought to escape, and had already found an outlet to leave the Temple, when a Roman soldier, seizing her by one arm, tried to draw her along with him.

"Almighty God, in the name of thy Son, save me!" cried the wretched girl, as the soldier brutally pulled her after him.

God was not deaf to the appeal of the Christian virgin; for at the same moment, like a flash of lightning, a Jewish warrior overthrew the soldier and then drew the maiden and child towards the outlet from the Temple.

Anna turned her head towards her preserver, and with eyes swimming in tears was about to thank him, when he, recognizing her, exclaimed:

"You here, poor creature!"

The maiden had not strength to answer; emotion

8*

deprived her of speech, and she sobbed aloud as she pressed Daniel's hand.

"Save yourself, Anna! every moment's delay is dangerous!" cried the young man.

"I will not save myself unless you accompany me," answered the maiden.

A flash of exceeding joy lighted up Daniel's pallid features; but fearing that his beloved might fall into the hands of the Romans, he shuddered with horror; and pushing her towards the aperture, repeated:

"Fly! save Jonathan, and I will soon join you!"

Anna obeyed, and the warrior rejoined Simon of Giora and John of Giscala, who at the head of a few Jewish soldiers were endeavoring to cut their way through with the sword, intending to seek safety in the upper city.

Already the fugitives had nearly reached the port of safety, when Daniel was called by an Israelite who lay on the ground, wounded and apparently dying.

Urged by compassion, the young warrior kneeled beside the dying man, whom he recognized as the soldier who had bound up Joel's wound; an although he knew him to be of a perverse and cruel nature, he would not refuse him aid in his last moment. He bent compassionately over him to raise his head, but the soldier turned like a trampled viper, and suddenly half-rising, took from his bosom a dagger which he had concealed there, and wounding the young man, stammered as he breathed his last:

"It was not in vain that I swore your death!"

A torrent of blood poured from Daniel's wound. He fell beside the corpse of his murderer; and leaning his head upon his right shoulder, remained motionless.

Until evening of that day, which was the 10th of August of the year 70, and throughout the days following, the fire now increased and now decreased. So that soon nothing remained to mark the site of the Temple but a heap of stones, which served as a tomb to innumerable corpses.

Thus were verified the prophecies of the Seers of God: The daughter of Sion was left as a covert in a vineyard, and as a city that is laid waste; * and a small number of her inhabitants shall be saved from the sword, and from the famine, and from the pestilence, that they may declare all their wicked deeds among the nations whither they shall go.†

Jerusalem lay in ruins; and by the supreme will

---

* Isaiah i. 8.   † Ezekiel xii. 16.

of the Almighty, eight months before her destruc
tion, during the intestine struggles between the rival
parties of Vitellius and Vespasian, the Capitol was
likewise laid in ashes together with the Temples of
Jupitor Capitolinus and those of Juno and Minerva.

Thus in the short space of a few months were
destroyed the Roman Temple, the centre of pagan-
ism, and the Temple of Sion. Baleful augury for
the two religions: one of which was to fall annihil
ated before the Cross, and the other, wandering and
proscribed, was to preserve its remains until the end
of time, as a testimony to the truth.

Meanwhile the worship of the true Faith, founded
at the price of the blood of the only-begotten Son
of God, which, throwing down the idols, was to plant
the symbol of our Redemption upon the heights of
Mt. Sion and upon the summits of the seven hills,
was hiding herself in the depths of the catacombs
of Rome. Her ministers and her faithful, covered
with plebeian garments, concealed themselves in the
most unfrequented streets, and only a few years before had attracted public attention; and those who
were to transmit so holy a heritage to posterity, lived
in poverty and humility; but called upon to declare
their Faith, confessed it upon the rack, at the stake,
and under the axe of the executioner.

Thus, whilst the Temple of Jerusalem was destroyed, and the Hebrew worship remained deprived of its priesthood, its altar, and its country, the Christian religion, rendered glorious by the blood of her martyrs, grew daily in the Eternal City, where the first Vicar of Christ had established his Sea and had died upon an inverted Cross!

CHAPTER XVI.

THE WANDERING JEW.

ALTHOUGH the Temple was destroyed, the upper part of the city still remained standing; and the surviving inhabitants seeking refuge therein, had taken up arms to defend themselves, though exhausted by hunger and divided by discord. But Simon of Giora and John of Giscala seeing all resistance to be useless, decided to capitulate, and in their blind folly imagined that they could dictate terms to the conquerors, whilst they could scarcely hope for grace from the well-known clemency of Titus. Nevertheless they demanded to be allowed to leave Jerusalem fully armed, carrying with them their wives and children.

Such audacity so exasperated Titus, that he immediately made ready for a final attack. The preparations lasted eighteen days, for it was necessary to raise the platforms to support the battering-rams which were to open the breach. About daybreak, on the morning of September 7th, he began the assault, and the setting sun illumined the ruins of Jerusalem. The words of Jesus Christ were accomplished: "Of the city of David not one stone remained upon another!"

The heads of the seditious party, unable to defend themselves, sought safety in flight; and finding no shelter, took refuge in a sewer, trusting to be able to remain concealed therein until the slaughter should be ended.

Meanwhile the Romans had penetrated into the mass of ruins, and like furious demons escaped from Avernus, committed so great and such cruel havoc, that my pen, weary of narrating so many sad scenes, is quite unable to describe it. I will merely say that Titus, pitying the fate of the vanquished, gave directions that they should kill only those who still offered resistance, sparing the unarmed and the women; but with all that the carnage was enormous. Woe to the conquered! for at all times and in every country it has always been difficult for the commander-in-chief to restrain his soldiery, who, accustomed to blood by long wars, seek to inebriate themselves with voluptuousness in the moment of victory; and was especially to that people which by 'ts wickedness has drawn down upon its head the divine anger, which sooner or later overtakes individuals as well as guilty nations.

Amid the flames, among the dead, bewildered by the frantic shouts of the conquerors, Anna wandered about in search of safety. Exhausted by so much suffering, she would have blessed the hand which might plant a dagger in her bosom, had it not been for Jonathan, whom Sara had confided to her care; it was for the boy she desired a place of refuge, but knew not where to find it; and walking aimlessly along, her face covered by a woollen rag which partly concealed her youth and beauty, hurried away from the spot where the butchery was going on; and now hiding herself behind some ruin to avoid being seen by a horde of the conquerors, and now quickening her steps, she reached the remains of a gate which she with difficulty recognized as that called of the Judges.

From that gate the road lay towards Calvary. Anna proceeded along the deserted path thinking that on the top of that mountain she would be in safety, and that perhaps Divine Providence had led her steps thitherwards; but she walked slowly, for she felt her strength failing, and was followed by Jonathan, who, although he had that morning eaten a large meal-cake given him by a charitable Jew, wept bitterly, asking for bread; whereupon she took him in her arms to hush his cries, and then seated herself on the ground to rest, but quickly rose at the sight of a man who at a few feet from her was climbing the winding path of the mountain.

The slow and equal step, the head bent upon the breast, led Anna instantly to recognize him; and hoping that he might guide her far from Jerusalem, resolved to join him. Raising Jonathan from the ground she quickened her steps; weary as she was, her breath failed her and she seemed to be, as it were, suffocated; at last she reached his side, but found it impossible to utter a word, and only a moan issued from her lips.

Then the wanderer turned his head towards her, and looking sadly upon her, took Jonathan from her arms and continued to ascend the sorrowful road towards Calvary.

Anna walked beside him, endeavoring to smile upon Jonathan, who was unwillingly borne along in the arms of the mysterious stranger, who in ascending to the top of Calvary turned pale and trembled convulsively, while large drops of cold sweat stood upon his wrinkled forehead.

Anna did not notice the emotion of her companion, for at that moment she thought only of the agony of that Divine Model who says: " Blessed are

they that mourn," in order that less bitter might be
those tears, the inheritance here below of every one
born of woman.

They had nearly attained the summit of the holy
mountain, when the mysterious man, placing the
child on the ground, ran to the top and fell there
prostrate with his forehead to the ground.

Anna also kneeled, but found it impossible to
pray; for her attention was diverted by the groans
of the stranger, who, with his face buried in the
earth, wept bitterly, uttering strange and incompre-
hensible words interrupted by sobs.

"The sins of that unfortunate man must indeed
have been great," thought the maiden, who, moved
to pity, prayed earnestly for him.

The mysterious stranger wept for a considerable
time; at last rising he said in hollow tones:

"After thirty-seven years of constant journeying
I am allowed to rest for one moment upon the spot
where the Lamb who taketh away the sins of the
world expiated my crime also!"

These words awoke Anna's wonder; and illy concealing her feminine curiosity, she asked him:

"Who are you?"

"Who am I?" replied the unknown; then added bitterly: "Listen to me, maiden, since I am

permitted to relate my crimes to a mortal being.
Listen, and do not shudder with horror, and do not
curse me . . . . . Born of an obscure family, I became a cobbler, and in my youth knew your father.
My lineage was humble . . . . My pride suffered
thereat ; so that instead of cobbling the sandals of my
fellow-citizens, I would have liked to lord it over
them. My mind was busied in silly projects, when
I heard men speak of a wonderful personage, who
astonished all by his miracles, and convinced them
by his words, preaching the love of the neighbor, the
contempt of riches, the forgiveness of injuries, chas-
tity, and self-abnegation. Many saluted him as the
Messiah expected from the Root of David, and proclaimed him King of the Jews ; others denied
him. I was among the latter and would not listen
to the words of the Just One born in a stable and
raised like myself in the hut of a mechanic ; and
when six days before Easter I saw him from afar
descending the Mount of Olives, and heard the joyous
shouts of the multitude who waved their branches
of palms and olive, saluting him as the Son of
David, my anger reached its climax, and a few days
after my sacrilegious voice, rising above all others,
shouted before Pilate's pretorium : *Crucify him !*
Crucify him ! . . . On that day in which the Im-

maculate Lamb was led to the sacrifice, I had put
on in sign of gladness a fresh doublet and new sandals, and stood exultingly upon the threshold of my
humble dwelling, before which the Son of God
was to pass ere reaching Calvary ... I saw him
dragging himself along with difficulty, bowed down
under the weight of the Cross.   When he reached
my house he tottered and put out his right hand to
steady himself against the door-posts.   Then in my
impiety I repulsed him, saying: 'Proceed!'   He
looked at me, and I read forgiveness in his glance.
But the Eternal Judge was watching to punish me.
At the same moment truth revealed itself to my
mind; but it was too late, for an inexorable voice
whispered in my ear: 'You shall journey until the
end of time.'   From that instant, driven onward by
some omnipotent power, I abandoned my house, left
Jerusalem and wandered throughout the world, but
without ever stopping for a moment.   Only when
one of my kind burdened with a heavy weight
passes near me, I feel impelled to assume his burden
and thereby to relieve him ...   For thirty-seven
years I have journeyed, and was impelled hither
that I might witness the destruction of my family
and my country; and typical of my people I now
return to my wanderings through the world, without

country and belonging to no nation. Alone and a wanderer I must walk until the end of time, until that final day in which, having expiated my crime, I may at last find rest." *

The wandering artisan ceased, and prostrating himself anew, continued weeping bitterly.

Anna looked at him in horror mingled with pity. His sins had truly been great and his punishment light, since it was only to last during this life; but reflecting upon its long duration, thinking that he would have seen generations born and die, cities rise from nothingness and become resolved into dust again; whilst alone, outlasting centuries, he would only expire with time itself, she felt great compassion for his fate, and prostrating herself in her turn, wept and prayed for him. She remained some moments with her forehead bowed to the ground; then rising, sought vainly for the wandering Jew; he was already far in the distance . . . the walker of centuries had again resumed his journey.

Left alone with Jonathan, Anna descended the hill of Calvary, deeming herself unworthy to remain in

* May I be pardoned for introducing into my story the poetic and popu-
ar legend of the artisan of Jerusalem, which is perhaps only a type of
the Jewish people ; but I cannot certainly be accused of having imitated
the French novelist, who makes of *The Wandering Jew* the hero of a modern
romance, which has no other aim but that of calumny and defamation.

that sacred spot; and sitting down on the side of the mountain, watched the ruins of Jerusalem, thinking that that heap of stones covered the remains of Sara, of Joel, and of Daniel.

Not knowing where to seek shelter, she decided to pass the night where she was, intending, when the frenzy of the conquerors was somewhat calmed, to go in search of Titus, and ask him for help and protection; for deprived of friends, of relatives, and of money, she had no other resource, and was unwillingly constrained to ask pity from the destroyer of Jerusalem.

It was not the first time that the maiden had passed the night in the open air; in that spot she felt herself secure, and in imagination saw an angel watching over her.

The darkness became momentarily more intense, the agonizing screams of the vanquished were heard from afar, and the echoes of the mountain repeated them. The stars shone brightly in the firmament, the air was warm and perfumed, for the smells of Jerusalem did not reach thither. Natura alone seemed tranquil amidst the terrible havoc, and the groans of the oppressed did not trouble her so.emn calm.

Anna, holding the sleeping Jonathan on her knees,

looked fixedly at the firmament, thinking ovei the
last words which her dying father had said to her:
" Look at the heavens, my daughter, and you will see
them sprinkled with numerous stars which you
could not count, but which surpass this world in
size; they all revolve through space, guided by the
hand of the Supreme Maker of all things; look at
the insect which drags itself on the sand of the
desert or through the slime of the lake, and you
will see that it contrives to find nourishment. Can
you believe, then, that He who watches over those
splendid worlds and takes care even of the little
insect, will forget the child of the man who trusted
in Him ? "

Remembering these consoling words, Anna took
no thought for the morrow, hoping that God, who
had preserved her through so many dangers, would
have care over her; the more so since according to
the divine word : " Sufficient unto the day is the evil
thereof." Besides, the hope of seeing Daniel, who,
she thought, might perhaps have been taken prisoner, gave her renewed courage; therefore praying
with her eyes turned towards the summit of Calvary,
she waited with patience until the dawn of the following day, which might possibly prove a herald of
better days.

CHAPTER XVII.

THE DEPARTURE FROM JUDEA.

THE maiden, seated on the ground, was sleeping heavily, when about daybreak four Roman warriors reached the summit of the mountain, whence they intended to witness the rising of the sun.

One of them, separating himself from his companions, halted at a short distance from them, with his eyes fixed upon the ruined city. It would seem that, like the Jews, he wept over the burning of the Temple, and over the destruction of so much magnificence, which the sad necessity of war had annihilated. He, however, was the conqueror, and by his orders the catapults, the balistæ, and the battering-rams had spared nothing; but the heart of Titus was naturally compassionate, and the obstinacy of the rebels had alone constrained him to such severe measures, so that instead of glorying in his dearly-bought victory, he bitterly regretted it.

After looking for some time, with eyes filled with tears, upon the ruins of Sion, which from that height appeared in their full horror, he perceived

Anna, and without recognizing in her the young maiden of the shores of Lake Asphaltites, moved only by the pity awakened in his heart at the sight of the pale emaciated girl, he gently drew near her the better to observe her. Anna then awoke, and springing hastily to her feet looked wonderingly at Titus, who, recognizing her at once, said to her, gaily:

"I thought you were dead, and am delighted to find that I was mistaken."

"Oh, Cæsar! enable me to find some refuge for this boy, who has suffered during the siege far more than I have," answered Anna, pointing to Jonathan, who timidly hid his face amid the folds of his adopted mother's garments, not daring to move, being terrified at the sight of so many strangers.

"Poor innocent child! you are paying dearly for the sins of your ancestors," began Titus, as deeply moved he caressed the curly head of Sara's son; then ordering the maiden to follow him, he silently descended the slope of Calvary.

When they reached the Roman camp, Anna was sent to the tent of Bernice, but she was not allowed to see her, for the king's sister was weeping over the fate of Jerusalem; but she found Flavius Josephus, who, succoring the wounded Jews, consoling the pris-

9

oners, or interceding for those condemned to death, was running hither and thither with the most bitter agony depicted on his countenance. Anna was delighted to see him, for she had believed him to be dead; but was unable to speak to him, greatly as she desired it, hoping to hear some news of Daniel.

For many days the maiden nourished the fallacious hope of seeing her childhood's friend, and inquired of him from the prisoners, who could give no account of him; but when she found that he was not with Simon of Giora, who, tracked to his fetid hiding-place by the Romans, had been forced to surrender himself, hope partially abandoned her, and entirely vanished from her heart when she heard that Simon himself was taken prisoner.

The celebrated chieftain had been seized, after having performed a ridiculous comedy, which was powerless to save him. Issuing by night from among the ruins of the Temple, he had sought, under the appearance of a spectre, to terrify the Romans; but the latter stopping him, and finding that they had to deal with a man of flesh and blood, and not with an impalpable spirit, angrily dragged him to the camp, when Titus ordered that his life should be spared, in order that he might appear chained to his triumphal chariot on the day on which the

conqueror of Judea should make his entry into
Rome.

Such a punishment, which in our own day would
seem cruel, was considered very light at that time,
in which every conquered enemy was forced, heavily
loaded with chains, to follow the triumphal victor,
to serve as a trophy to his conqueror, and as an object of scorn to a nation rendered proud by the continual victories gained by its banners in every part
of the world.

Anna, in the fulness of her sorrow, not only wept
over the supposed death of Daniel, but also mourned
over the misfortunes of her country, from which
probably she was to be forever separated. And
who would not have wept over such ruin, and over
the fate reserved to that nation which formerly
called itself the elect of God ?

Although the heart of Titus was magnanimous
and pitiful, still he could not prevent the cruel butchery of the Jewish prisoners, whom the Romans murdered to get rid of them.

To divert his soldiery from further carnage, Titus
gave orders that they should throw down those remains of the Temple which had been spared by the
flames, as well as the entire city, with the exception
of a portion of the enclosure of the western wall

and the towers of Phasælis, Heppicus, and Mari-
amne, which yet remained standing; and then pass
the plough over the spot formerly occupied by Jerusalem, as a sign that the rebellious city should never
again be rebuilt.*

The prisoners of war amounted to ninety-seven
thousand, and were divided into several classes ;
those of higher rank were reserved to follow the triumphal cortege of the victor; those who were not
yet seventeen years of age were sold, together with
the women and children, at a very low rate.   Divine
Justice !   The Son of God had been sold for thirty
pieces of silver, and thirty Hebrews were sold for
one piece of the same money !   Many were destined
for the circus and the amphitheatre to serve as gladiators ; the rest were sent to labor in Egypt.

Sad was the fate of that nation ; notwithstanding
a very few years after it again endeavored to raise
its head ; but in vain, for divine wrath had decreed
that it should never more form a distinct people,
nor yet fusing with the conquerors, but were to remain isolated, without country, without an altar, and
without a priesthood, and to bear testimony throughout future ages to the truth which they had denied.

* The Roman laws forbade to rebuild those conquered cities over whose
site the plough had passed ; notwithstanding that, the Emperor Elias Adri
anus rebuilt Jerusalem, giving it the name of Elia Capitolina

Jerusalem being destroyed, Rome anxiously awaited the victor, to whom the Senate had decreed the honors of a triumph; but winter being near at hand, Titus would not quit Judea; but leaving one of his legions to guard the wretched ruins of Sion, he repaired to Cæsarea, where he gave several shows, in which many Jewish slaves perished in the circus struggling against gladiators more expert than themselves.

From Cæsarea Titus set out for Berytus; and attracted by the delights of that city, he remained there during the winter, and at the opening of spring set sail for Italy.

Agrippa, Bernice, and Flavius Josephus followed the Roman leader; and then Anna, mingling among the hand-maidens of the king's sister, left Judea. Weeping bitterly she bade a final adieu to the land which contained the bones of her ancestors, and where she had grown up beside Daniel. Without other care or affection save that inspired in her by the orphan boy, deprived of friends and relatives, a slave and destitute of means, she set foot in a strange land, condemned to live upon the hard bread of exile, where even tears are more bitter than those shed in one's native land. Afflicted and despairing she would have sought death had she not been

fully convinced that sooner or later all sorrow ends
with the termination of this mortal life. Resignation, the daughter of Faith, gave her strength to
live; so that when she reached the city of Romulus,
she wept no longer, but bowed her head resignedly
to the supreme will of Him who humiliates and
exalts, condemns to tears and destines to glory,
without man having the right to demand a reason
or to rebel against his inscrutable decrees.

CHAPTER XVIII.

ABOUT mid-day on the 10th of August of the year 72, the second anniversary of the destruction of the Temple of Jerusalem, three boys were playing under the portico of a house of noble appearance situated on the Quirinal, not very far from the spot later occupied by the Baths of Diocletian.

The statues of·the ancestors of the patrician to whom the house belonged, stood upon colossal pedestals under the arches of the porch, alternately with the rich spoils and trophies gained in the wars against the barbarians. In the centre of the atrium stood a vase of *guallo antice*, into which the water poured in torrents from the mouth of a dolphin of parian marble.

The three boys wore the toga prætexta, the ordinary garment of the sons of patricians, with the golden tulla, indicating youth, hanging from their necks, and were playing at *turbo*, a sort of top of pointed form which they spun round by means of whips.

Two of them were apparently about ten or eleven years of age, and seemed to be twins, so alike were they in looks and stature. The third was somewhat older, and his pale thin features and deep black eyes gave him an expression of precocious gravity.

Without the portico, not far from where the boys were playing, a little slave sat on the ground, exposed to the full rays of the burning August sun, having before him a basket filled with dates, and was selecting the ripest and placing them in a silver vase. He was naked to the waist, and wore no clothing save a large white woollen band wrapped around his loins, and hanging down over his knees, leaving the rest of his legs bare. Looking merely at his profile, he might have been taken for a bronze statue, so brown and regular were his features. Entirely intent upon his occupation, he held his head down, and only occasionally looked anxiously at his young masters, who were laughing and making a tremendous noise.

The fate of the Roman slaves was cruel beyond all belief. The slave possessed nothing. All his property belonging to his master, he was not looked upon as a man, but as a thing destitute of free will. The slaves were bought and sold like animals; sometimes even they were hired or lent out. Their master with a woman had not the legal force of matrimony, and not only their owner, but any free man, might torment or murder them with impunity. Contempt and want of the slightest consideration for those poor wretches was so greatly in vogue, that Cato the Elder, that model of Roman virtue, said: "There is no other distinction between a slave and an animal, except that the former is obliged to render an account of his actions to his master."

"Lucius has won!" cried one of the boys, seeing that the top of his sickly-looking companion continued to spin, whilst the other two had turned upside down.

The boy named Lucius did not answer. Going up to the pedestal of one of the marble statues, he took thence a piece of silver money which was lying upon it, and was intended as the prize of the winner of the game; then running towards the little slave who was selecting the dates, he handed it to him, saying timidly:

"Take my winnings, Jonathan; I have no need of money; my good mother gives me all that I require."

"Neither do I need it," replied Jonathan, haughtily rejecting the money; then immediately repenting of his pride, he took it, saying in a low voice:

9*

"I will give it to the old man Hezikiah, who has been blind for more than a year, and who needs i more than I do."

"You are good to all, poor Jonathan! but all are not good to you," said Lucius, as he returned to his former station under the portico.

Meanwhile the twins had run to Jonathan's basket, and filling their hands with the dates, eat them greedily, throwing the kernels into the face of the slave, who, trembling with rage, could with difficulty restrain his tears.

"How cruel you are! I will not play with you any longer!" cried Lucius, wishing to prevent his companions from tormenting the poor child.

"You call us cruel because we amuse ourselves with this slave! But were not slaves born to divert their masters? You ought to know that, since your mother has so many," answered one of the twins.

"My mother says that slaves are men as well as the patricians, and would punish me severely did I dare to ill-treat them. But you are cruel, and I am going away to avoid the sight of your barbarity," added the gentle Lucius, turning his back upon th ill-bred boys, who stopped him, saying:

"Remain, and we will no longer molest Jonathem, but if you leave us, we wil. revenge ourselves upon him."

Lucius remained for a moment undecided, then turned a compassionate glance towards Jonathan, who, unable longer to restrain his tears, was sobbing bitterly; and fearing that the two brothers might carry their threat into execution, returned to the game; but after spinning the top a few times more, he leaned against one of the columns, saying:

"I will play no longer; Jonathan shall take my place; I will lend him my *turbo*, and give him all my winnings."

"Yes, Jonathan shall play with us, and if he loses we will beat him," exclaimed one of the twins, dragging the trembling slave into the porch.

Jonathan took the *turbo* and made it spin. The little patricians imitated him.

"Jonathan has won!" said Lucius, who assisted at the game as umpire.

"No!" screamed the infuriated twins.

"He has won; he has won!" repeated Lucius.

"Do you not see that my *turbo* is still spinning," added Jonathan, unwilling to lose the game.

"Peace, vile slave!" said one of the brothers, aiming a severe blow at Jonathan, who, unable to support the injustice and outrage which were done to

him, forgot for a moment his servile condition, and
pushed away the one who had struck him, and
would even have returned the blow had not Lucius
interfered.

In falling the boy had hit his head against the
pedestal of one of the statues of his ancestors, and
slightly injured his forehead.

At the sight of the blood his brother ran into the
house, and soon returned accompanied by a matron
sumptuously attired.

"Come to my dwelling, for if you remain here
they will kill you," said Lucius, endeavoring to drag
Jonathan after him; but it was too late! for the
matron seizing the culprit by the hair, cried out in
a voice rendered harsh by anger:

"Hebrew viper, do you dare strike the son of
your master?" Then without noticing the wounded
boy, who sat on the ground weeping more from anger
than pain, ordered two slaves to tie Jonathan to a
column and to beat him until the skin was torn
from his flesh.

Lucius uttered a scream of horror on hearing this
inhuman order, and finding that he could do nothing
to save his protege, hurried from the spot.

One of the slaves bound Jonathan to the column,
raised his hand armed with a leathern scourge, which,

falling upon the naked shoulders of the Loy, left a bloody furrow.

Jonathan gave an agonizing howl, and already the hand of the slave was raised to repeat the blow, when Anna, who had heard the boy's screams, rushed up, and placing herself before him, kneeled down, and extending her arms beseechingly towards the patrician, implored mercy for her little charge.

" Be quiet, and do not annoy me with your cries," said the matron.

"Oh, scourge me in his stead! My limbs are stronger and can bear the blows better," persisted Anna.

" Peace!" answered the mistress, coldly.

" You have not, then, the heart of a woman!" exclaimed Anna, blinded by sorrow.

The patrician made an angry gesture, then ordered the slaves to tie up the maiden, and to scourge her as well as Jonathan.

The order which condemned the daughter of the Asmoneans to be scourged by the hand of a slave was about being carried into effect, when a woman of commanding height and sad yet gentle aspect, entered the porch, leaning her hand upon the shoulder of Lucius.

At the sight of her visitor, an expression of dis

may passed over the face of the patrician, who, hastening to meet her, said, with ill-concealed contempt:

"I did not expect a visit from you just now, Portia."

"I know it, and am aware that my presence is unwelcome," answered Portia, smiling sadly; and pointing to Anna, added: " As usual, I come to ask for pardon."

The patrician bit her lips until the blood came; and becoming pale and red by turns, began thus:

"When as girls we dwelt in our father's house, I bowed my head to your will, and in spite of myself yielded to the influence which your gentle, and at the same time obstinate, character exercised over mine; now I am a wife and mother, and the absolute mistress over my servants. I do not repair to your house to give you advice which has not been asked of me. You can murder your slaves, and I will not open my lips to prevent it; therefore imitate my example, and do not meddle in my domestic affairs."

" When I can raise my voice to ask mercy for an unfortunate creature, or to advise my father's daughter to be less inhuman, I should think myself guilty did I remain silent. Oh, Faustina! have pity upon that woman, who like yourself was born free, and is perhaps, like ourselves, of illustrious lineage."

"What do I care for her lineage? Bernice gave her to me, and in exchange I presented her with my finest jewels. Her boy has wounded my son; she has insulted me, and now I will punish her according to her deserts."

"That poor child is not so guilty as you think. Lucius told me the whole affair," resumed Portia.

"Lucius thinks like you, and you educate your son in a manner unworthy of a Roman patrician."

"I am not educating him for this world, where man has no right to oppress his fellow-man," replied Portia, caressing her son's head with maternal tenderness; then turned her eyes towards Anna and made a gesture of surprise at seeing a wooden cross attached to an iron chain which hung from the slave's neck.

At that sight Portia's countenance changed its expression, and its usual gentle sadness gave place to an air of resolution, and turning to her sister she resumed:

"That woman must not be tortured; and if you will not yield to the voice of humanity, you shall at least bend to that of your caprice . . . You have fre-

quently begged me to give you my villa at Tuscu-
lum, and I have always refused to sell it to you, because that spot is dear to me, my husband having
died there. Well, then, cede to me your rights over
that slave and her boy, and I will give you my villa
in exchange."

Faustina looked wonderingly at her sister, thinking that she had become crazy, for it seemed impossible to her that for two slaves she could yield up so
delightful and healthy a dwelling-place. Then she
said :

"You have lost your senses; a thousand times I
have offered you a fair share of money in exchange
for your villa, and you have constantly refused it,
although far less wealthy than myself; and now
you are willing to deprive yourself of it merely to
gain two abject slaves !"

" It is true that hitherto I have not wished to sell
you that place so filled for me with sweet and at
the same time sad remembrances ; but my dying
spouse left me his wealth, recommending me to give
our son examples of mercy towards the poor. In
yielding up to you my villa in order to sweeten the
existence of two unfortunate beings, I accomplish
his wishes."

Faustina remained silent; her sister's generosity

had greatly moved her, and for a moment she was almost tempted to give her the slaves without accepting the villa in exchange; but her emotion lasted only for an instant, and quickly gave place to the egotism of the capricious and inhuman woman.

"Well?" asked Portia, anxiously.

"Every one to his tastes," answered Faustina; "and since you prefer the company of two slaves to your delightful dwelling, I, for one, will not oppose your choice. Take the woman and the boy; I will take the villa. The contract is made."

"It is made," answered Portia, who herself untied the cords which bound Anna and Jonathan, whilst Faustina withdrew to escape the sight of the joy of the slave, whom she would willingly have had scourged to death had she not longed so ardently to possess her sister's villa.

Anna could not find words to express her gratitude. Speech too frequently is inadequate to portray the sensations of the mind; and a look, a pressure of the hand, or a tear, are more eloquent than a long discourse.

"Poor child, in my house you will no longer be a slave!" said Portia, in tender tones.

Anna tearfully kissed the hand which pressed her own, and quickly followed the benevolent mat ron into the house which opened its hospitable doors to receive her—the haven of safety where she was to repose after so many tempests, and in which happiness was to dawn upon her for the first time after so long and such cruel trials.

CHAPTER XIX.

In Portia's house Anna's days passed away less sadly. The matron was a Christian and scrupulously followed those dictates of the gospel which com mand man to love his neighbor, especially the needy and the unfortunate; and when she had performed some benevolent deed, she felt quite happy in the thought that her deceased spouse was blessing her in heaven. Her house contained no slaves, but only zealous and affectionate servants, who forestalled the wishes of a pious and charitable mistress, who treated them as it were like brethren.

Anna had quickly gained Portia's love by means of her sweet, gentle character, and by the recital of her numerous trials, so that the good patrician cherished her like a daughter, and endeavored to make her forget the sorrowful past. But the memory of former days was ever before her mind, embittering the present; for when we have suffered much, the soul rarely yields to joy, and even in the midst of e joyment luxuriates in a hidden melancholy.

Anna was not happy, although she saw Jonathan's future fate secured. He no longer went about
half-naked like the slaves. but dressed like the sons
of free men, and was the companion of Lucius in his
studies. She was not happy, because she thought
continually of Daniel; and the remembrance that
he had died in error, bitterly grieved her, since it
ensured her being separated from him, not only in
time, but also throughout eternity.

Portia led a very retired life, never repairing to
the theatres nor public shows; going out merely to
assist at the Christian assemblies which were held
in the Catacombs.

One day, as the matron and the young maiden
were returning from one of those reunions, they
determined to go to the Palatine Hill, where the
Jewish slaves were laboring at the construction of
the new colossal amphitheatre erected by order of
Vespasian. They went there to see if it would be
possible to assist some of those unfortunate creatures,
who, poor and enslaved, eat their bitter bread of
servitude bathed with the tears forced from them
by the cruel treatment of the Ædiles* and the
inferior superintendents of the public works.

* According to Varro, the Ædiles derived their name ab ædibus ; and
among oth· ·duties, had the charge of overseeing the shows and the public
works.

An..a had never before been in that quarter. She walked sadly and silently beside the matron, who was to her more a friend than a mistress; and when she stood before the palace of the Cæsars, which from its magnificence was called "The Golden House"— *Domus Aurea* —she shuddered at the sight of the new building, which towered in the distance.

Passing the palace of the Cæsars, the two women turned their steps towards the vast square containing the foundations of the colossal edifice, and found the place encumbered with carts, conveying immensely large masses of stone ; and mingled among the carts, multitudes of slaves passed and re-passed laden with large pieces of tracestone, which they could hardly carry upon their shoulders. The greater part of those slaves were Jews, and were taciturn and morose. Poor creatures, they had good cause ! A baleful silence reigned throughout that spot ; and in truth the amphitheatre which they were building was also baleful, for its arena was to be watered by the blood of so many martyrs !

Anna's heart beat with anguish at the sight of her fallen countrymen, who with foreheads bathed in sweat, and worn out by fatigue, passed near her ; and unable to restrain her tears, waved the unfortu-

nate beings a salute, and said a few words of comfort
to them in their native tongue.

The circumference of the ellipsis of the vast edifice
was finished, and they were already working at the
second line.   The building, however, went on slowly,
owing to its immense size.

The two females had stopped before the principal
entrance of the amphitheatre, and Anna turned her
head towards two Hebrews whose pallid and emaciated features and bleeding shoulders inspired her
with pity.   Absorbed in that sight, she did not perceive a cruel scene which was taking place on the opposite side from that where stood the two Israelite
slaves.

A gray-haired old man was hurrying towards the
building, laden with a large piece of tracestone which
weighed down his aged shoulders.   As he was about
entering the amphitheatre a youth accompanied by
an overseer was coming out; and at the sight of the
old man, he stopped, and offered to relieve him; but
immediately the *superintendent* raised the leathern
scourge armed with iron points, which he always carried with him, and struck the naked back of the
slave, crying angrily: "Do not meddle with others,
but let every one bear his own burdens."

The slave shuddered from head to foot, uttered a

hollow groan, and instantly seized his superior by the throat, intending to make him pay dearly for his cruel blow; but the other overseers hastening up, forcibly attacked the rebel, who, struggling vainly, fell to the ground overpowered by the number of his enemies.

Anna, disturbed in her meditations, turned her eyes towards the prostrate man, and, pale as death, screamed aloud in desperation at recognizing Daniel, who lay on the ground still struggling violently.

"Portia, save Daniel! save thy unfortunate friend!" exclaimed the maiden, crazy with the fear of witnessing the death of her lover just at the momen when she had discovered him after mourning for him as dead.

The matron, not knowing from whom to ask pardon for the culprit, and hearing the Ædile, who just then came up, sentence Daniel to be scourged, trembled with horror, and sought to drag the maiden from the fatal spot; but almost instantly halted at the sight of Titus, who, clad in the triumphal toga always woven with threads of gold and purple, and proceeded by the Lictors, was advancing towards the amphitheatre.

Seeing the conqueror of Judea, whose clemency was known to all, the matron took courage, and running towards him, began to say, while bowing respectfully before him :

"Titus, the widow of a Roman patrician begs to speak with you."

Titus courteously saluted the matron, who in solemn and dignified tones proceeded :

"Son of Cæsar! if your clemency be not a phantom and your justice a lie, save from cruel punishment an unfortunate slave, guilty only of pity towards an old man."

"I do not understand you!" said Titus, wondering at the matron's words.

Then Portia related the occurrence, and again interceded for Daniel.

Titus was silent ; but the expression of his youthful face portrayed the emotion of his heart; then turning towards the Ædile, he reproved him severely, and ordered him instantly to loose the slave, to whom he said kindly :

"To honor and relieve old age is the duty of all. You did well! And I, in reward of your good action, will grant you your liberty." Then taking from the hand of the Ædile the ivory rod, laid it upon Daniel's head, saying : "You do not belong to me, but the Senate will not refuse the freedom of one slave to him who has conquered so many.

Go, you are free, according to the right of the quirites." *

A shout of applause broke from the crowd ot captive Jews who had witnessed the scene. Although Titus had been the principal cause of their slavery, they could do no less than admire his clemency.

Daniel stood petrified as it were with wonder. The generosity of the destroyer of Jerusalem had humiliated him almost as much as the blow of the overseer; but quickly recovering his natural haughtiness he turned to thank his benefactor, but it was too late, for Titus had already departed, forbidding any one to follow him.

Daniel then turned towards the matron, and was unable to contain himself at the sight of Anna, who held out her hands to him, weeping for joy.

It would be impossible to describe the rapture of the two friends who had endured so much, and who now met so unexpectedly in a strange land. But Daniel's joy vanished when he remembered that he had been struck in the presence of the two women. That thought profoundly humiliated him. And what heart would not suffer deeply at seeing itself outraged before its dear ones.

* This was the formula by which freedom was conceded to slaves.

10

But Anna had understood Daniel's uneasiness, and said, quickly :

"When insulted and scourged by our oppressors, you seemed as noble to me as on that day when I saw you fighting on the walls of the Fortress Antonia."

Daniel did not answer, but thanked the maiden with a smile which was far more eloquent than words.

"Follow me, my children, and under my roof you can give full vent to your joy," interrupted Portia.

The two young people obeyed her, and as they followed the matron, who hurried away from the amphitheatre, Daniel told Anna that having been wounded he had been carried to the Roman camp ; and that, thanks to his youth and strength of limb, he had been carefully cured, in order that he might become a gladiator.   And Anna, in her turn, informed him that having been brought to Rome among the handmaids of Bernice, she had been presented by King Agrippa's sister to a cruel matron, who would have had her scourged to death, had not Portia generously purchased her.

"The adorable will of God has reunited us in a foreign land," said Daniel, in tones of emotion, after the young maiden had ended her story.   "Oh ! let me always live by your side; an exile and poor, I have nothing to offer you; but I am free, thanks to Titus; and to procure your support, my strong arms shall labor like those of a slave."

"A promise binds me; I cannot become the wife of a Jew," replied Anna, in a tremulous voice, and lowering her eyes filled with tears.

"I have been a Christian in faith since the day on which I saw the Temple destroyed!" exclaimed Daniel. At these words, an expression of ineffable joy passed over the young girl's features. Such felicity seemed to her like a dream. Then she realized that she had not trusted God in vain; she felt the good effects of filial obedience, and heartily blessed Divine Providence, who by such wonderful ways had led her to the enjoyment of the happiness which she had so long and so ardently desired.

EPILOGUE.

A YEAR had passed away since a Christian priest had blessed the union of Anna and Daniel. The two spouses no longer lived in Rome; for Portia had repaired to Palestine to dwell in the land sanctified by the death of the Son of God, and had taken a house at Jericho, together with her friends.

The climate of Judea suited the feeble health of Lucius, who became daily more attached to Jonathan; so that the affection of the two boys, maturing with their years, changed into a firm friendship.

Anna and Daniel were happy—as happy as they could be on this earth, where nothing is perfect and durable.

Every year, on the anniversary of the destruction of the Temple, the two spouses repaired to Jerusalem to visit the spot where the redemption of mankind had been completed. Only on that day were they allowed to approach it; for the Jews who still dwelt in the vicinity of the ruined city had only obtained that permission by dint of long and urgent prayers. On that day, writes an eye-witness, an en tire nation goes up to weep bitterly over the ruins of Sion. Mourning women, and gray-haired old men with their garments rent in token of sorrow, wept over the remains of the Temple, and the legionary on guard demands a tribute corresponding to the time which he allows them to indulge their grief.

Daniel and Anna did not weep over the ruins of the Temple, but prayed upon the top of Calvary; and in the fulness of a grateful heart, the young wife thanked God for the happiness which He had granted her, supplicating Him likewise in favor of her oppressed brethren; and remembering the arti-sau who had related to her his sad story, prayed that the wandering traveller, after the lapse of ages, might find pardon and peace in the bosom of eternity.

www.ingramcontent.com/pod-product-compliance
Lightning Source LLC
Chambersburg PA
CBHW030128030726
47498CB00007B/2609